THE CONFERENCE ON BEAUTIFUL MOMENTS

JOHNS HOPKINS
Poetry and Fiction

John T. Irwin
GENERAL EDITOR

THE CONFERENCE ON

.... THE JOHNS HOPKINS UNIVERSITY PRESS

RICHARD BURGIN

BEAUTIFUL MOMENTS

BALTIMORE ....

This book has been brought to publication with the generous
assistance of the G. Harry Pouder Fund.

The Johns Hopkins University Press
2715 North Charles Street
Baltimore, Maryland 21218-4363
www.press.jhu.edu

Library of Congress Cataloging-in-Publication Data

Burgin, Richard.
  The conference on beautiful moments / Richard Burgin.
  p. cm. — (Johns Hopkins, poetry and fiction)
  ISBN-13: 978-0-8018-8518-1 (acid-free paper)
  ISBN-10: 0-8018-8518-3 (acid-free paper)
  ISBN-13: 978-0-8018-8519-8 (pbk. : acid-free paper)
  ISBN-10: 0-8018-8519-1 (pbk. : acid-free paper)
I. Title. II. Series.
PS3552.U717C66 2007
813'.54—dc22   2006010571

A catalog record for this book is available from the British Library.

My thanks to the editors of the following publications, in which
these stories first appeared: *Antioch Review:* "The Second Floor";
Confrontation: "Vivian and Sid Break Up"; *Pleiades:* "Mayor Bat"
and "The Conference on Beautiful Moments"; *TriQuarterly:*
"Cruise" and "Jonathan and Lillian"; and *Witness:* "Dates in Hell,"
"Duck Pills," "Robert and His Wife," and "Uncle Simon and Gene."
  My special thanks to Edmund de Chasca, Bella Gurevich,
John T. Irwin, Barbara Lamb, and Robin Theiss for their invaluable
help with this book.

For my friends who have helped me so much recently and especially for my beloved son, Ricky, who will always be my best friend.

Contents

THE CONFERENCE ON BEAUTIFUL MOMENTS

JONATHAN AND LILLIAN

One couldn't really say that Lillian's dinner parties had attained legendary status primarily because her guests (rarely more than nine and, on this evening, seven) were generally discreet, talking about them mainly to each other. There were several reasons for their unusual discretion. First, at any given party half the guests were as famous, or nearly as famous, as Lillian herself and for them to meet other celebrated people was in the natural course of things. Also, Lillian didn't have dinners exclusively for theater and film people like herself but always had writers, musicians, or painters, and sometimes even businessmen and lawyers, among her guests. Consequently, there was no one circle in which news of the parties circulated widely. The lawyers and businessmen talked about them the most perhaps.

Still, there were any number of people in show business or the arts, or simply moneyed people who knew about them and yearned to be invited to Lillian's—people for whom such an invitation would be the crowning touch of their social year or even decade. To see the inside of her storied Santa Barbara house in the mountains was itself an achievement. Then to be able to talk with her and her famous friends and to eat the exquisite food invariably prepared and served by Santa Barbara's finest caterers was something one might never experience anywhere else. Moreover, there was the sense of history in the paintings, sculptures, and especially the signed photographs of all her friends that adorned the walls. Here was Picasso, there was Judy Garland, Elizabeth Taylor, Barbara Streisand, and Tennessee Williams, and at the table writers and directors of the first magnitude—it all made one feel slightly dizzy if one were one of the less-celebrated guests, and there were always a few of those people at Lillian's dinner parties too.

Finally, Lillian had the inestimable gift of making people feel happy with themselves, so they had little desire to gossip maliciously about her. Nearly everyone thought she was among the nicest people they'd ever met, certainly the nicest famous person they'd ever met. As a result, people truly enjoyed themselves at her parties. They arrived looking as good as they could and stayed as long as possible, giving her goodbye hugs and kisses more heartfelt when they left than when they had arrived.

How strange that he was now one of Lillian's guests, Jonathan thought while driving to the party. Of course, as her latest biographer (the biggest commercial break so far in his writing career, in which he'd published only one largely ignored novel and two modestly successful biographies) it was not so wildly strange, he supposed. What was far stranger was that he was apparently going to become her lover—at least she had unam-biguously invited him to stay and spend the night with her after her other guests went home. However, there was still the question of her guests and whether he would pass his audition with them. The way she had struc-tured things, he thought this evening clearly represented his coming-out party, where her Hollywood friends could meet and access him. No won-der he had to take an extra swig of Mylanta before leaving.

It was only a five-mile drive from his little ground-floor apartment on West Valerio Street to Lillian's mansion. He began driving up State Street, the glass-enclosed street lamps casting soft light on the succession of elegant restaurants and dress shops, fitness centers, and banks. They all seemed to merge together as if connected by the lights and flowers—hi-biscus, birds-of-paradise, azaleas, and bougainvillea—and by the mag-nolia and palm trees. He saw the clock tower of the courthouse bathed in a lemon-colored light with people standing on the outdoor balcony looking at the city and at the ocean and mountains. Then, as he started driving uphill, he saw El Encanto, the hotel in the mountains where she'd taken him to lunch on their first meeting. They had eaten outside, where the view of the ocean was spectacularly unobstructed, but he'd been too nervous to notice. He'd overdressed and drunk too much and felt he'd said too little. Nevertheless, after little more than an hour she'd asked him where he was staying.

"In a hotel on State Street."

"But dearest, I meant where is your home?"

"In New York, in Queens actually."

"An apartment?"

"Yes."

"So you flew here to see me?"

"Yes, I did."

"Well that won't do," she'd said, finally removing her sunglasses and revealing her violet-blue eyes, a startling contrast to her sun-yellow hair. He'd nearly gasped. How could a woman her age look that stunning and young?

"You need to live here, I think, so we can have the kind of talks we've had today in a way that will be convenient for both of us."

"That would be great but . . ."

"Don't worry about the money, that would only get in the way of the book. I'll get you an apartment in town while you're working on it, OK? But please don't look so concerned. I hope you don't think I'm trying to seduce you and will end up asking you to stay with me. I know you writers need your space."

He mumbled a thank you and forced a smile to show he understood her joke, and she smiled back playfully but somehow seriously as well. He remembered then that she had a reputation for having affairs with younger men, both in and out of show business, which these days was something of a trend in Hollywood. It helped him accept what appeared to be happening between them but he was nervous nonetheless. He had never met, much less flirted with, someone of her stature. He felt he'd had very little success or even excitement in his life and now was suddenly being flooded with both.

"Will that be OK?" she'd wanted to know.

"Of course it's OK. It's incredible really, how kind you are."

"I find I don't spend much time in LA these days. I barely use my house in Beverly Hills anymore. I far prefer my Spanish getaway home in the mountains, where . . ."

"It's beautiful."

"Yes, it's beautiful. Here, it's still beautiful. You understand that," she'd said, as if his understanding of the obvious were an achievement. "I'm so happy they suggested you to write the book. I think you're an artist—that you have the soul of an artist. I liked the novel you published, too. I did my own research on you and I think you're an artist, and that's the kind of person I like to work with and get close to."

He'd thought for a moment that something might happen that day, but it didn't. When lunch was finished they walked slowly through the hotel gardens and then, in front of her Mercedes, she leaned forward and brushed against his lips, her blond hair almost tickling his cheeks. She told him they would meet at her house in a week—she had to go to LA first on business—then gave his hand a quick squeeze and disappeared into her car where her driver was waiting.

During that week he'd tried to stay focused on his book and not attempt to predict the future but she began calling him every day.

"I want to take care of your hotel, so I'm going to give you my credit card number and have you put it on my card."

"No, that's not right."

"Don't be silly, Jonathan. It's only fair. You didn't expect to stay this long and I won't have the time to get you an apartment till I get back."

"I don't know," he mumbled.

"I do. So that's settled."

He began thinking a lot about the next meeting at her house, where she'd insisted on inviting him for dinner when it could have been for lunch in a restaurant. Dinner at her home did have definite connotations that he couldn't deny. Was she planning to sleep with him? Was she waiting for him to make the first move?

Yet it didn't happen that way. First, she surprised him by addressing the issue before the caterer had even brought the main course into her vast, candlelit dining room—a room so large it seemed like a little section of Spain itself.

"You're quite a *young* man to be writing my biography, but you don't write like a young man. I think that's the best combination, don't you? Maturity in art, youthfulness in appearance. At least I've often been attracted to younger men. My philosophy is, if the man *is* younger I promise to *look* younger." She laughed and he quickly joined in. "Tell me, how old are you, Jonathan?"

"Thirty-eight," he said, slicing three years off his age and immediately regretting he hadn't said thirty-seven.

"That's a good age, Jonathan, very good. Do you think you can handle it if I start to fall for you, like I think I already am? And do you think I'll look young enough for you?"

"Oh yes. You look younger than me and, of course, infinitely better."

"Thank you, angel. When you come to my dinner party Saturday night why don't you plan to stay with me afterwards?"

"That would be wonderful," he mumbled into the salmon salad he'd just been served.

"I hope it won't jeopardize your ability to do the book . . . objectively," she said with a slight smile. He felt frozen and didn't respond, the book suddenly seeming so far away and almost incidental.

"I know," Lillian said. "When we make love we'll use one part of our brain and when we work on the book we'll use the other, OK?" she said, laughing again. "Does that sound reasonable?" she added, extending her hand, which he immediately clutched, then held for a few seconds.

"Sure, it sounds great."

"I don't know about you but I *always* have to be in love. If you're not in love with someone and sleeping with them life is just kind of ridiculous, don't you agree?"

He nodded, not knowing what to say.

"Marvelous, then it's settled."

A minute after leaving her home, however, he chided himself for his passivity (the same kind of passivity he used to show toward his ex-wife) and for having lost yet more control over his so-called unauthorized biography. Still, the main thing he felt that night and for the next few days before her party was a dreamlike excitement that made it very difficult to sleep. After all, he was about to become Lillian Glass's lover, which seemed almost impossible to believe, and she had also said she was falling in love with him—or had he imagined that?

Lillian's Spanish "getaway house" had twelve bedrooms and extensive grounds filled with water fountains and flower gardens, and a vast swimming pool overlooking the Pacific. Jonathan rang the bell then took a deep breath. A few moments later Kenneth, the butler, opened the door—a good-looking man in a black tux, who was tall and blonde like everyone else in Santa Barbara and who gave him a friendly smile that was a nice, unexpected stroke for his ego.

Lillian, dressed in black herself, except for a yellow silk scarf (the approximate color of her hair), met him in the living room. "Hello darling," she said, kissing Jonathan ardently on the mouth. "I'm so glad you could come early."

"You look beautiful, you're amazing," he said, pleased that for once he meant every word of a compliment.

From his position in the hallway Kenneth watched them as closely as he could, especially Jonathan, before going into the kitchen again. Look what she's settling for now, he thought with a snicker. This new one was almost frumpy and dull-looking with his ill-fitting glasses and receding, thin brown, will-less hair, ten years older, at least, than him; also shorter, less muscular, with a face not even in the same universe as his.

Perhaps Jonathan thought writers could get away with looking like that, and maybe they could in New York. But this was Hollywood, where a man didn't get any points for looking five months pregnant. Worst of all, perhaps, was how uncomfortable he looked wearing a tie when the whole point of dressing up, of dressing at all, was to feel sexy and to show it. Could Lillian possibly become his lover? Could one actually have sex with someone like Jonathan? Tonight would probably be their big night. Lillian liked initiating her new lovers on a party or premiere night, something to help her remember them by and give the occasion more sentimental value. Even a project like Jonathan could be useful that way with enough work. Eventually, with some new clothes and other beauty aids, she could erase the way he truly looked as if he'd never appeared in the world that way before. It was merely a question of money and Lillian had plenty of that. She had spruced him up too, Kenneth remembered. He still wore the clothes she'd gotten him, though he'd had to integrate them slowly into his wardrobe lest Gina get too suspicious.

He finished his inspection of the refrigerator and closed the door. Amazing how Lillian, how all people repeated themselves, were slaves to their behavior, though they thought themselves so free and au courant. Lillian had saved him for a party, too, although he'd had to cater it. Tonight he was the headwaiter and would be paid well (better than Lillian realized, he thought, with another smile). Though she eventually dumped her "civilian lovers," that is, the younger nonstars, Lillian did treat them pretty well financially. But, he didn't like thinking of that. It didn't make the plans for tonight any easier to carry out.

His cell phone rang then from inside one of the pockets in his tuxedo.

"Shit," he muttered, and then quickly discovered that at least the call came from a pay phone.

"What's going on?"

It was Hummel.

"Everything's OK."

"Anyone there yet?"

"Her boyfriend, that's all."

"Is he going to stay?"

"Don't know. Probably. He won't be any trouble."

"Why's that?"

"Trust me, he's a real wilted dick. Why are you calling?"

"Don't worry, it's not trouble."

"That's not the point. They could subpoena my phone. There'll be the history of all the calls I've gotten on it then. They can do that now. So if things don't work out they could . . ."

"Things are going to work out and the phone company has the records, not the phone, but get rid of the phone anyway—one less piece of potential evidence."

"I'm not gonna make it on the cell. I'm gonna make it on a pay phone in Santa Barbara. It'll take three minutes longer, maximum, that's all. I'm not negotiating this. I won't put it on the cell. I won't risk that."

"Good. Then throw out the phone after you call me. Drown the fucking phone, OK? I'll get you a new one."

Shit, he said to himself, after the call ended. He hated to get rid of the phone; he hated to get rid of any gift—especially one from her. He heard steps, then saw Lillian.

"Everything going well?" she asked. She always got so nervous before these dinners, though she'd done so many of them.

"Everything is perfect."

"Perfect?"

"Couldn't be better."

"OK then," she said, winking at him as she walked out to the hallway to meet Jonathan.

"Everything looks dazzling," Jonathan said and Lillian smiled.

"Kenneth does a marvelous job."

"Was that Kenneth who let me in?"

"Yes, quite gorgeous isn't he? And he's very loyal. Let me show you what we did with the dining room," she said, taking his hand as they walked into it.

"It's magical," he said. "I never realized how many paintings there were before, or how much light."

On the table were more candles in glass holders than Jonathan had ever remembered seeing. The lights half lit the paintings on each side wall. Again he told her it was beautiful and she gave his hand another squeeze.

"I finished chapter four last night, about your early Broadway years. I'm really kind of pleased with it."

"That's wonderful, angel. Oh, the bell rang—Did you hear it?—the bell rang. The guests are coming, the guests are here," she said, leaving him in the room of paintings and photographs and ubiquitous candlelight. Jonathan looked at the shelves and the candles and thought he'd arrived at a strange moment of happiness, that his life had had hideous frustrations to be sure (thinking of his failed career as a novelist and of his being childless), but that he was happy now in this moment at least, and Lillian always preached that only the moment is real.

He moved out of the dining room into the hallway and saw Lillian embracing Alex Hornstein, the renowned divorce attorney, and his current wife, Kathy, who looked like a model. He noticed that Hornstein continued to hold hands with her while talking to Lillian. This will not be an easy night, Jonathan thought. It was never easy to be not only the least wealthy man at a party but also the least charismatic. To see and feel one's true station in life, one's essential obscurity, was, he supposed, the inevitable result of attending one of Lillian's dinner parties. Denial could only go so far, he thought with a little smile, as he looked out shyly at Hornstein, a man at least four inches taller than he was, with a head of convincingly full black hair and a deep confident voice, which he modulated with supreme skill during his frequent TV talk show appearances and undoubtedly also in bed with his blonde, outrageously attractive wife.

The bell rang again. Kenneth opened the door and Jonathan recognized Eric West, the movie director, who only a few years ago had won an Academy Award and who at the start of his career had directed some of Lillian's best movies. He had a silver goatee and long silver hair and wore a tie and sports jacket, but also his trademark blue jeans and black cowboy boots to enhance his western image. Though he'd grown up in New Jersey and lived mainly in New York and Malibu for the past thirty years, West had been born in Arizona, or so his bio claimed, and he continued to promote himself as "the cowboy director." With him, sporting a huge diamond ring he'd given her when they married last year, was Louise Leloch, the young actress. She was West's fifth wife, by Jonathan's count, and one of his youngest. As Jonathan recalled, she'd appeared in supporting roles in West's last two movies.

Jonathan just had time to finish a vodka and tonic before shaking hands with Hornstein and Company (for an attorney he had quite a macho grip) and then with West and his wife. Then a minute later, Jonathan saw the revered novelist Margo Garret, with her good friend the gay art gallery owner Maurice Germand.

"Ah, the Great Garret," West exclaimed, turning away from Jonathan to kiss her on the lips. Immediately Jonathan remembered that West had directed at least two movies based on Garret's novels and that she had co-written the last screenplay with him. The movies had done well at the box office, too.

"Eric!" she said, taking his hands, her cheeks coloring slightly after he kissed her.

"This is Louise, fire in my loins, my sin, my soul, Louise—the Great Garret, who deserves to win next year's Nobel Prize, and every year's for that matter."

Jonathan was impressed that West knew Nabokov as well as Fitzgerald, but he had said it with such grandiloquence that Jonathan cringed. Neither Louise nor Margo seemed the least bit embarrassed, however, as they quickly exchanged kisses on each other's cheeks and talked about how absurd it was that this was their first face-to-face meeting.

Without any discernible announcement, Lillian's guests suddenly began moving to the living room, with its enormous array of art and its grand view of the gardens and the ocean. Jonathan sat on a chair in the corner by the picture window that overlooked the rose and tulip gardens, where he soon accepted a new drink from Kenneth. He took a few sips when a thin, balding man with piercing blue birdlike eyes stood before him.

"I'm Maurice Germand," he said, extending a hand.

"Jonathan Trantnor. I've been to your galleries many times and, like the rest of the world, admire them greatly."

Maurice inclined his head a little like a swimmer trying to shake water out of his ear and smiled slightly. "Thank you . . . You're going to write a biography of Lillian, aren't you?"

"Yes, I am."

"How lucky for you, and her too, I'm sure. Lillian is so divine, I just love her to death."

"It is lucky for me—a great piece of good luck, especially since she's being so kind to help me with the book."

"Lillian has always taken an interest in people who write about or photograph her," he said, with what Jonathan thought was a slightly ironic smile. He felt a sudden tinge of embarrassment, took another sip of his drink and said, "I think it's one of her gifts to be interested in nearly everyone she meets. That's why so many people become her friends."

Germand nodded and Jonathan felt he'd recovered nicely.

"Every time I come to Lillian's," Maurice said, "I feel like I'm coming to a familiar but rather fascinating gallery . . . of people as well as paintings."

"A gallery or a museum," Jonathan said. "The range of people that she knows is extraordinary."

"Because she, herself, is so extraordinary. Do you know if she sees Peter these days?" Maurice asked, referring to Lillian's son, who lived in Santa Cruz, as a part-time eco-terrorist, most-of-the-time pot dealer.

Jonathan, somewhat surprised that *he* was being asked this question said, "Not recently, I don't think."

"That's a shame. I think he took the divorce very hard and then got in with some bad people."

"Yes, it's a real sadness in her life, but Lillian is strong and keeps positive about Peter, keeps hoping."

"He's still a young man," Maurice observed.

. . . .

At dinner, Jonathan was seated next to Kathy Hornstein on one side and Louise Leloch, Eric West's wife, on the other. The food—chicken, fish and pasta, a delicate tomato salad, and two kinds of wine—lived up to its reputation, the conversation less so. At least at first. No one topic dominated the table for any length of time; instead everything seemed skittish and a little forced. It reminded Jonathan of an acting troupe improvising from audience suggestions in fitful one- or two-minute spurts before moving on to the next suggested topic. Finally, the guests found something to talk about that interested them all—the recent much-publicized wedding of the singer/actress Dana Russell.

The Hornsteins asked most of the questions and Lillian and West, who were at the wedding with Margo, gave most of the answers. Jonathan, making a mental note to not entirely recede into the conversational background, asked some questions too.

The wedding and reception, which a thousand people attended, had been filmed for a future television show and was covered by much of the nation's (and a good deal of the world's) media. When one movie star found out that a television show was involved she apparently changed her mind and decided to go at the last minute, but demanded, and apparently

received, a hundred fifty thousand dollars to attend. She arrived, looking in the words of West, "pale, bloated, and horribly depressed." Margo
agreed that the actress did have "the worst taste in the Western world.
What a paradox to have all that beauty clothed in such glaring trash."

There were stories and jokes told about Michael Jackson and Elizabeth
Taylor, and there was the anecdote about the two actresses who'd had a
fight thirty years earlier. One approached the other at the reception to
make up only to have the other turn her head and walk away. All the stars
were referred to by their first names, and Jonathan was not always certain
who was being discussed, though he'd immersed himself in show business lore since getting the book proposal. Tuesday and Liza he knew, of
course, but which Janet were they referring to, which Gary?

Then the discussion turned more to the celebrities at the reception
who were ill and to speculation about who might not live long. The brief
moments of hilarity were replaced by a somber mood, which got considerably darker when they began discussing what they had been doing on
9/11.

"I was writing," said Margo. "I didn't find out until afternoon. And
then I worried about my friends who worked near there and I started calling frantically, but by then it was impossible to get through."

"Was anyone you know hurt?" asked Jonathan.

"A friend of mine who worked at the World Trade Center . . ."

"Yes, Paul," said Maurice quickly. "He unfortunately didn't make it."

"I'm sorry," Jonathan said, "that's awful."

Margo bit her lip and said, "It was very sad, very cruel."

"Margo wrote a beautiful poem about it that the *Atlantic* published,"
Maurice said.

"No dear," Margo said, "it was actually published in the *New Yorker*."

More testimonies and condolences followed until they led to an uncomfortable silence. Then West began describing a Hollywood birthday
party he'd been to that was thrown by a famous director.

"I heard that was a huge party," Lillian said.

"Yes, lots of people, lots of rooms. His house is really extraordinary."

"Does he still supply cocaine to anyone who wants it?"

"I didn't notice any coke, but I'll tell you what I did notice," West said, with a twinkle in his eyes. "I walked into one of the guest rooms to use the john and there was no less a star that Brian Kove doing something very strange to some model or other, I think, and damned if he didn't go right on with it. I think he was giving her an enema and dicking her from behind at the same time."

A couple of the guests laughed uncertainly.

"I mean he didn't even stop when I walked in. Just turned his head and looked right at me and continued till I left."

"Darling, you probably made his day," said Lillian.

"You probably made him come—which I understand isn't that easy for Brian," said Maurice.

"I mean, I've heard of Hollywood decadence," said West, "but this was ridiculous."

"I know an actress who had an affair with Brian sometime last summer," said Louise. "You know who I mean, Eric, and she told me that all he ever wanted to do, besides watch his own movies, was play games with enemas. Enema love he called it."

A few more guests laughed.

"Well there you have it," said Lillian to West, "the idea for your next movie."

"Yes," said Eric. "Adultery and drugs are old hat. Everything has to be anal these days to be up to date."

"It's the new intimacy," said Hornstein, clutching his wife's shoulder.

Everyone laughed again, including Jonathan, who managed to force a laugh as he squirmed in his seat wondering just what his future with Lillian held for this evening and beyond.

· · · · · · · · ·

Ridiculous to still be thinking about the phone on this of all nights, Kenneth thought, but it seemed he couldn't help it. He could feel its weight inside his jacket as he served and removed the plates and glasses and tried to avoid any meaningful eye contact with Lillian, who had already smiled at him once. It was not as if it were a little animal he was getting rid of. It was a mineral, he guessed, or at any rate inert, not alive. So why think about it? But given the kind of mind he knew he had he wasn't really surprised. Sometimes he thought of his mind as a department store with a series of specialty sections each devoted to torturing him in a unique way. Once he wandered into one of these sections there was nothing he could do to get out except let the thoughts the section had stored up have their way with him.

She had given him the phone right after the first time they'd slept together so she could call him whenever she wanted him. It was her first gift to him and he used to stare at it, sometimes even with Gina, and say, "this is the phone where I'll get my first part, talk to my first agent, get my first deal." Lillian had said she'd help him (hinted at first, but then said it after their second or third time) and she was one of the most powerful women in Hollywood. "With your looks and body you've definitely got a shot. I'll put you in touch with people, angel, don't worry, they'll be impressed when they see you."

But I can act and I can write too, he used to say to himself, while they were having sex. And I'm actually a better actor than you, he'd think then in an angry, defiant voice that came from another part of the department store that he couldn't stop, could only hope to control by not saying it out loud, for example, while he was coming.

One time he did tell her about his acting, about studying at an actor's studio, and he made her listen to him. He read the part of Tom from *The Glass Menagerie* right in front of her wall-length mirror. She'd praised him, of course, though it was impossible to know if she meant it. Yet she *had* done a few things—introduced him to a couple of producers and directors, arranged for an audition. Nothing big, probably just the minimum one would expect from a woman in her situation. He did get a small part in a commercial from it—just a few words, but it paid well—and then work as an extra in two movies. But then it all stopped. She ended their sessions and with them the career favors and, of course, the clothes as well. Then the parts stopped, the agent that she'd gotten for him no longer returned his calls, and even Gina said he should leave the business. "It's eating you up," she said to him tearfully in bed. Then she went on to cry even more as she started talking again about wanting a child, something that was still unthinkable to him.

Lillian's final gift was the offer to be her butler/handyman, somehow even more humiliating than the hustling and small-time drug dealing he used to do—but she paid well so he couldn't even say no to that.

The guests were through with dinner and had returned to the living room, where the painting was. Even the choice of it, a Diego Rivera, was inspired, since seven others in that room alone were certainly worth more. Recently he'd made a point of talking about art to Lillian so she'd know he knew the value of things. All this would help deflect suspicion from him, would make it look instead like the work of a bungling burglar who passed up a Picasso and a Renoir for a Rivera.

He walked in with the tray of cognacs and noticed Louise Leloch talking to Jonathan. In her tight, low-cut yellow dress she was showing to maximum advantage her perfectly positioned breasts and ample honey-blonde hair, neither of which was probably real, but still, he decided to serve the guests around them and to listen to them talk for a moment, while sneaking in a look at Louise whenever he could.

"So you two met about the book and then it just clicked between you big time, huh?" she said. "I mean, the word is that she really likes you."

"I hope so," Jonathan said shyly.

"Anyway, your book will make you immortal because Lillian is immortal."

"Thank you, that's nice of you to say, but I really don't think so."

"But why?"

"I don't think anybody's writing will make them immortal, least of all mine. I know a lot of writers think so, but I think that's just an illusion. I think everyone's art and movies and novels will simply, eventually, be forgotten. You know, I had an editor friend, an editor, you see, not a writer, who once said to me, 'Art is the last illusion,' and I think he was right."

"Art is the last illusion," Louise repeated, "I like that."

"If these artists are so hung up on immortality, I think having children is a much more direct route, a much better solution."

"I sure wish Eric felt that way. I've been trying to convince him to get me pregnant for a year now. Course he's had so many children already, but couldn't he give me just one more?" she said laughing. "Do you have any children Jonathan?"

His face reddened.

"No, I'm sorry to say I don't. I wanted to, very badly in fact at one point, but my ex-wife didn't. I used to even have dreams in which I'd be talking to my son only to wake up and discover that I'd just had a dream. But no, my ex-wife was really married to her work, and since then there hasn't really been an opportunity."

"What did she do?"

"She was a novelist who *really* wanted to succeed and would pay almost any price to do it. I don't think writers like that mix very well with babies."

There was an awkward silence until Louise finally said, "Well, I think it's great and really romantic about you and Lillian. That's the way it was with Eric and me, too. I was just a bit player in one of his movies. I think I said ten words in the picture, but one day during rehearsal our eyes just met in a special way and he invited me to dinner that night and then— boom—we just clicked. So, yuh, I was crazy about him right from the start but I also had a lot of hang-ups and insecurities about dating a man who was so world-famous and, you know, older."

"But they all went away, obviously. The hang-ups."

"Not completely," she said, laughing, as she finished her drink. "I mean, you see the nice breasts but behind them beats the heart of a hick."

Jonathan laughed and spilled some of his drink, and Louise laughed too, holding his wrist for a few seconds as if to steady him.

"Excuse me sir, I'll fix that," Kenneth said, removing a cloth from his tuxedo pocket which he kept for this purpose and dabbing away at Jonathan's jacket. He bent down and attended to the rug, catching a glimpse of the Rivera painting on the way down and for a nano-second on the way up.

"Thank you very much," Jonathan said.

"You're welcome, Sir."

Kenneth lingered a little longer, enough to hear Louise add, "But seriously, it gets better, it does. I mean once I went to bed with him the age thing went away pretty quick. And the other stuff, well, that maybe takes a little longer. We've been together almost three years now and I still feel in awe of him."

Then Kenneth saw Lillian giving him her version of a dirty look, and he returned with his tray to wait in the kitchen for the guests to leave. It would take one of the confident ones to start the process, then the others would all leave within ten minutes. Perhaps it would be Margo, "the great Garret," as West had called her. Regardless who it was, he would have to spring into action and fetch their coats with a convincing smile firmly in place. Later Lillian would pay him in cash, telling him to take the key to open the gate and return it tomorrow. But he'd refuse, saying it made him uncomfortable, and ask her instead to open and close the gate electronically—as if he didn't know or want to know the code, which he'd already given, along with copies of the house and gate keys, to Hummel. He also left a living room window unlocked so it could look as if the burglar had made a daring climb over the gate by tree, landed in the yard, and entered through the window. Yes, he had definitely done his homework.

Lillian, of course, would be hysterical, at first. He would have to spend some time with her and the police too, probably, which would be nerve-wracking and difficult. He couldn't even spend the money right away either, but eventually if he kept his cool he *would* get it (he'd tell Gina that he'd won it gambling) and then, in a few months or so, they could leave. That was the thought to focus on, leaving Southern California, the world capital of lies and illusions, which had turned him into a hustler and a slave, where he'd once had to let men suck him and where he'd even sometimes had to get on his knees and suck them, too, while pretending to enjoy it. He had only to think of that, the old fat smelly men and young pimply boys he'd done it to, to know that tonight was right and was the only thing left he could do.

. . . .

She was at the door, head inclined slightly, a beautiful slope to her neck, thanking Kenneth for his impeccable job in a voice that was breathy but thrillingly refined. Jonathan watched her, feeling like a child who beholds and invents his mother at the same time in a moment of rapture so pure it is almost like terror. He thought, she is truly magnificent; maybe my era of meaninglessness, of being thwarted in everything, is over.

She had turned toward him, the door closing behind her as she embraced him.

"Lillian, it was the dinner party of all dinner parties."

"Thank you, angel. I was waiting so long for this moment when you'd finally hold me. I thought it would never come."

He could feel her trembling slightly against him and her need for him; the incongruous coexistence of her confidence and vulnerability excited him enormously.

They walked into her room holding each other around their waists.

"Let me use the bathroom to take my face off and get ready for you," she said. "My face is only meant to be viewed until midnight."

He laughed, loud enough for her to hear because he knew she liked to hear him laugh, and lay down on the far side of her enormous bed. He saw the light go on in the bathroom. Around him were more paintings and photographs of Peter—her only child, as far as he knew. He could feel the Viagra he'd taken (just in case) coursing through his system, already working. God bless those greedy scientists. It was funny how people went to the theater or looked to writers like Margo, who'd been divorced four times, for wisdom, but it was the scientists alone who could really make life better for people, who were really the only hope.

He waited and waited, barely able to contain his excitement as he continued to sculpt his erection.

"Here I am, darling," Lillian finally said, emerging from her bathroom in a flowing yellow silk robe. She lit two pale candles and then shut off the lights.

"Did you have a good time at my party?" she said, as she snuggled against him.

"I had a wonderful time. The pasta was incredible. All the food was."

"And did you like my friends?"

"They're great—quite an amazing group of people. I didn't get to talk a lot to everybody, of course. I talked mostly to Kathy and Louise."

"I noticed. You were very animated, not at all as shy as you predicted you'd be."

"No. I guess I wasn't. I surprised myself."

"But not me."

"They're both very down to earth. Both really easy to talk to."

"What were you talking about so passionately? I was starting to feel a little jealous. I mean they're both so ridiculously good-looking and have those perfect bodies that I've never had and never will have."

"You're kidding, right?"

"About what?"

"Being jealous."

"Not really. Not entirely."

"Well, I mean that's ridiculous."

"So what were you talking about? Something *ridiculous* too?"

"Kind of. Actually, it was a bit philosophical with Louise. We talked about values, believe it or not."

"Did she also talk about babies? Baby Present talking about Baby Future?"

"Yes, she talked about wanting a baby."

"Since she married Eric she's been like a walking commercial for the joys of motherhood, although she's never had one as far as I know. So were you babied to death?"

He laughed. "In a manner of speaking." They were quiet for a few seconds. He was puzzled by her rare use of sarcasm and by her quasi-admission of jealousy on this of all nights and wondered if they would end up making love after all, since it was very late. He decided to say nothing. Let her wonder about him for a moment. It seemed it was always the other way around, his always trying to guess her mood and please her. She who had had such a full life that his own life was now devoted to writing about it.

"Would you like a drink, darling, to re-cheer you up?"

"Sounds nice," Jonathan said.

"I have a little surprise for you in the refrigerator. There's a bottle opener and some glasses on the counter that Kenneth left for us. Why don't you bring it in, sweetheart?"

"Good idea. I'll be right back."

He felt happy and excited as he walked toward her kitchen, which was larger than some of the apartments he'd lived in. On the counter were the glasses and bottle opener on a tray and inside her enormous refrigerator was a bottle of champagne—Dom Perignon, no less—with a pink heart-shaped card that read "For us, my Jonathan." He read it three times, feeling as if he were tasting the champagne already.

On the way back to her room he heard some unsettling noises, the kind of noises that a person hurrying and carrying something clumsy would make, but decided not to say anything to Lillian. Not when his consummation was at stake with his first, and undoubtedly last, world-famous celebrity, the incomparable Lillian Glass.

. . . Some things worked out well, others not as well. Despite his anxieties, he opened the champagne bottle well, nothing substantial spilled, they laughed, they drank and kissed—it was their happiest moment. His lovemaking, on the other hand, was more pedestrian than he would have hoped, and he had no one to blame but himself—he'd just been too intimidated to be spontaneous. She'd certainly been generous to him, saying all the right things and more, but he didn't think she enjoyed it very much except when he finally allowed himself to come. Still, nothing catastrophic had happened, which is essentially all you could hope for the first time.

Afterwards he lay next to her holding her hand, which was nice. They were silent for a minute. He asked her a question then realized she was sleeping and softly, almost politely, snoring. He got out of bed, picked up a candle, and carried it to the bed, and stared at her. She looked strangely innocent with her eyes closed, her face older looking, of course, without her makeup but still extraordinarily beautiful and mysterious. He suddenly felt ashamed of his spying, returned the candle to the bed table and lay down next to her. The biggest mystery to him was why she wanted him.

Suddenly she opened her eyes and stared right at him.

"Are you all right, angel?" she said.

"Yes."

"I dreamed you were looking at me, were you?"

"Yes, I was."

"Was it all right what you saw?"

"Of course, it was beautiful. Go back to sleep." She shut her eyes again.

"Please don't look at me like that again. I told you I'm not to be viewed after midnight—certainly not without my makeup."

"I'm sorry. It was stupid what I did."

"Will you promise not to?" she said with her eyes still shut.

"Yes, absolutely."

"People are so alone when they sleep."

"I know."

"They're alone when they're awake too, but it's worse when they sleep. All their fears multiply, mine do anyway. I think about Peter and many things. Sleep has never been an easy thing for me. It's like the hardest part I have to play and really I can't play it at all, not without help from my pills or from whomever I'm with, angel, because the slightest thing can ruin it, do you think you understand?"

"You can trust me never to do it again."

"So really, in spite of everything, when you looked at me you saw something that was maybe a little beautiful?"

"Something a lot beautiful."

"That's why we'll be together—don't you think—because you see something beautiful in me and I do in you, too. Isn't that the truth about us?"

"Yes, I think it is."

"Oh thank you, angel. I love you," she said, closing her eyes again.

"I love you, too," Jonathan said.

· · · · · · · · · ·

The phone rang. It was Hummel.

"It's over," Hummel said. "It's all over."

"No interruptions?"

"For a second I heard someone walking."

"Shit!"

"Don't worry, they didn't see anything. It was probably her new screw getting a drink or something but nothing happened. It's all good. Relax."

"OK. Get rid of your keys and your phone."

"Get rid of yours, too," Hummel said.

"I'll call you tomorrow from my new one. Adios."

Kenneth opened the window and screamed into the wind, surprised to discover it was misting. It was a happy scream, like he used to feel when he scored a touchdown in high school or when Gina did him just right. Well, he wouldn't be playing football anytime soon but he could celebrate with Gina when he got back to their apartment in Oxnard. They hadn't had sex in a long time and besides, that way he wouldn't have to explain anything because he knew she'd sense something and start asking questions. She always did. The only thing that could keep her from talking about it was if he started making love right away. He reached into his coat pocket, withdrew a Viagra and swallowed it. A half hour from now when he got home it would already be working.

Suddenly he felt a panic about what he'd done, as if the wind had blown it into him. He shut the window. He was in the department store again wandering through unfamiliar aisles trying to find the exit sign. Immediately he began reviewing the arguments in his favor. She didn't know he had a key or knew the security code. He'd refused to take the key from her. Also, he had an alibi for when he wasn't working, which the mileage in his car would confirm. He'd been driving home from work. The collect call he'd make to Gina as soon as he left Santa Barbara would prove that. Finally, the loss of the Diego Rivera would only lower her collection a million or two and was undoubtedly insured anyway. No one would be hurt by this. Even the cops would soon be bored.

Ten miles later he spotted a pay phone in Carpenteria and called Gina collect.

"It's me. The party's over."

"Is everything all right? You sound weird."

"I'm fine. Everything's fine."

"How was the party?"

"Typical."

"Was Eric West there?"

"Yuh, he was there."

"Will you tell me all about it when you get home?"

He promised he would. She loved hearing about all the movie stars he waited on—what they were wearing or talking about. Then he said, "Listen to me. When I get home I want you naked except for your leather jacket and I want you on your knees in bed."

"Really?"

"Yes, really. I'll be there in twenty minutes, maybe twenty-five," he said as he realized he still had to dispose of the key and the phone. There was a strip of sand and then the ocean about a hundred yards in front of him with no one in it. He may as well do it now.

Things were getting better, he could already feel the wind that had been roaring inside him diminish to a kind of manageable buzz. By the time he did Gina and had a glass of wine he'd be out of the department store. He pictured doing her from behind again, imagining he was Brian Kove. He could already feel the first tinglings of his Viagra. So what if he sometimes thought of her as a young boy? So what if he'd imagined Lillian sometimes as a man too. Who had to know? He didn't have to impress *himself*, did he?

He kicked off his shoes, took off his socks, and rolled his pants up to his knees, looking around himself as he walked straight ahead into the water. First he threw away the key but held the phone a little longer. Goodbye Queen Lillian, goodbye Hollywood, he said to himself. Anyway, you couldn't really have a career that meant anything if you died, it was an illusion to think you could. He knew that now. You couldn't have anything, not even a phone, because knowing that you would die drove you crazy, just knowing that you and whatever work you did would completely vanish. He threw the phone as far as he could, watching it sink instantly like a pebble. Lillian knew the same thing as he did—it was one of the secret things they had in common. It was why she kept distracting herself with new lovers like Jonathan, he thought, and with making one movie after another. Workaholics and careerists were just people who couldn't bear thinking. Just addicts like everyone else, only with the Good Housekeeping Seal of Approval.

The black water was surprisingly warm and inviting. It, too, was addictive—maybe the most addictive part of God's department store (the master pusher who wanted to addict you to the whole universe). The only difference was He always got His way or at least always called you in. Maybe he'd surprise God for once and come back to His water soon, on his own terms. Come back for good and rest from everything, 'cause the water wasn't an illusion—it was wet and when it was ready it could fold over you forever.

THE SECOND FLOOR

"Happy Birthday, the snowman, or Cary Grant?" the woman asked from behind the counter, holding up the stamps as if they were jewels he might want to examine.

"If I say Cary Grant, will you think poorly of me?" he said.

"Excuse me?" she said.

"The Snowman," he said, to say something. "Give me ten snowmen." He had always been jealous of Cary Grant anyway and hardly needed the reminder. While he was waiting for his change the rotund, red-faced woman in the line beside him was presented with the same choice by her postal clerk. She hesitated a second, blushed, then said "Cary Grant" in an illicit-sounding half whisper.

Outside a strong wind was blowing in the blue sky. When he was a kid, not much younger than Abby he supposed, he used to think the wind controlled the color of the sky. There were blue winds, and gray winds, and multicolored winds, which produced the colors of sunsets and rainbows. Of course, since the wind does move the clouds it wasn't a completely false notion, he thought, the moral being it's as difficult to be completely wrong about something as it is to be completely right. He'd actually tried to talk about this to Abby once but she couldn't really grasp it or else wasn't interested.

Abby and he had had three conversations so far, four if he counted the first one when they met in the park. He'd always needed someone to talk to—a simple enough need, one would think, but in practice surprisingly complicated. The park, where he'd met her and where he'd gone today with the expectation of meeting her again, was in a lower-class part of Philadelphia. There were some swings (half of them broken), a dented, graffiti-laden slide, a metal jungle gym, and a dirt path that led to a pond. Unfortunately, the pond had largely dried up and its banks and what was left of its water were heavily littered. It was by this pond that he'd started talking to Abby. He never asked her if she came to the park on any specific days or at any particular times, but it seemed that at about 3 P.M. she was usually there. She wore jeans the first time that matched the blue in her eyes and a green top that matched the green that was equally prominent in them.

"I've never seen eyes like yours," he said to her on the first day.

She smiled. Her teeth were spaced apart a little and very white.

"It's like seeing two sets of eyes compressed into one."

"Is that good?"

"It's magical. It's like the beauty of blue sky and green grass. You have sky and land eyes both," he said, and she giggled.

At ten past three on a weekday in this park, most of the people were either kids skipping school (some of whom were playing basketball on the concrete court a hundred feet away) or people who were out of work. A few were probably also selling things they shouldn't be, though in an unobtrusive way, moving toward and away from potential customers quietly, as if they were clouds themselves.

He was the exception, he realized. He didn't work because he no longer had to, not since he'd inherited his share of the money from his father two years ago. Still, he chose to live relatively near the park just a couple of train stops away (or today a longish walk). It was really the best place for him to live, given how he had to live, where no one ever bothered him.

If Abby didn't come it would be a wasted day, he thought, looking at his watch. He sat down on a wooden bench with two half-rotted beams and looked out at the basketball court. One rim was bent and both baskets were without nets. It was like looking at a giant mouth with two teeth missing. What was he thinking by coming here, and yet what choice did he have? There were times like today, when the reality of the life he was living in his apartment became unbearable and he desperately needed to talk to someone. With Abby he could talk about almost anything. For example, he'd even told her about his mother.

"How old is your mom?" Abby had asked.

"Very old, Abby. So old that her brain isn't working right anymore, and she has to live in a special home."

"Oh," Abby had said solemnly, as if he'd told her a great secret, and since he'd never really talked about his mother to anyone else maybe it was a great secret.

Abby's mother worked and her father no longer lived with her. She said her school got out at 2:30 but he didn't believe her. As far as the length of school days was concerned, now they only got longer. It was because no parents were home from work at 2:30, nor could they afford babysitters. But he decided he wouldn't press her about this. Maybe it was just one class she was cutting, like gym, because she wasn't the athletic type. It was strange, he used to be the athletic type but that left him years ago. He had many memories, in fact, of coming to playgrounds and sitting on a bench waiting for basketball players to show up.

It was 3:23 when the girl sat down on his bench. He looked at her tight black skirt hiked high up her legs and her cheap, clinging gold shirt that was missing two buttons. She had a cigarette in her mouth.

"You got a match?" she said.

She probably had a tooth missing but he couldn't be sure. She had closed her lips over her cigarette very quickly.

"No, nothing. I don't smoke."

"That's healthy of you."

He didn't like the remark and shrugged, too boyishly, he thought. She was not that much older than Abby—certainly young enough to be his daughter and yet he felt almost intimidated.

"You waiting for someone?"

"Yuh, but I don't think she's coming. What about you?"

"You ain't a cop are you?"

"No. Hardly."

"You sure about that?"

"Yes. Completely."

"So what're you waiting for?"

"A friend. What about you?"

"Me," she said, tapping her chest with her index finger. "I don't even know how I got here. Ain't that a bitch?"

She laughed a little and he looked for the space in her teeth again but the cigarette blocked his view. Her face was pretty in a rough sort of way. It was a contradictory face framed by short black mannish hair with a little nose, big brown, oddly vulnerable eyes, a rough chin, and surprisingly thin lips.

"How'd that happen?" he said, looking around himself briefly for Abby again.

"Got wasted and never made it home last night. Woke up and thought 'shit, I gotta make it out of here,' so I walked out from where I was staying and came here. Only problem is, when I got out on the goddamn street I realized my money was missing."

"That is a bitch."

"I give the jerk a whole night and he rips off my ass."

"Where do you live?"

"South Philly."

"I could pay for your cab. You gotta cell phone, I'll call one."

"No taxi's gonna come here, but thanks mister. You're wearing some nice clothes. I can see you must be doing all right."

He thought he should say thank you but wasn't sure and so said nothing.

"I'm dying for some weed or a beer, anything . . ." she said, half to herself.

"I know what you mean . . . What's your name, by the way?"

"My name? My real name's Francine but everyone calls me Cincy."

"Are you from Cincinnati?" he said, trying his best to smile.

"Bingo. You?"

"My name's Jerome."

"No, I meant where are you from?"

"Oh, Philadelphia. I never traveled much."

"But you got the money to if you wanted, right?"

Her question stopped him short and made him wonder if she was the terminally nosey type.

"Yes, I guess I do, but I don't feel the need to travel."

"Why's that?"

"I have everything I need right in my apartment," he said, wondering if he'd already said too much.

"Oh yuh? That's a nice way to feel. I wish I could travel. You got any weed or crank or anything like that in your apartment?"

"It's possible. I have some things."

"Yuh, I bet you do. I bet you got a really interesting apartment. You feel like showing it to me?"

"I need to wait for my friend now. She still might come."

"Would I know this friend? Does she work around here?"

"No, no. You wouldn't know her. She goes to school, nearby."

"Oh, a school girl, huh? I never did too much of that."

"She's actually cutting school, I'm pretty sure, which is . . . disappointing. I don't know why she isn't here today."

"You know what they say, 'Girls just wanna have fun!'"

He forced a laugh but felt a flash of anger. She was trying to manipulate him. This Francine/Cincy was trying to hurt him, by making him doubt Abby, as if he wasn't suffering enough already.

"Hey, don't look so sad. Maybe she decided to go to school today."

"That's what I'm thinking. That's why I want to wait till at least four."

"So, you live far from here?"

"A few minutes."

"Why don't we go to your place and get high and then you can come back here by four?"

Her offer made him remember the strange look on Abby's face near the end of their last conversation. It was as if he'd said something that frightened her and her blue-green eyes looked scared and dazed and almost teared up. Maybe he *had* scared her and she'd decided not to come back to the park. He cursed himself for not knowing where she lived (he should at least have offered to walk her home once) or even knowing her last name. As a result, he might wait in the park forever and never see her again.

"OK, let's go," he said, thinking he should have done this with Abby a long time ago, and then everything would have been different.

They walked up the path past the swings and slide. A yell came from the basketball court. A boy had probably just scored a basket, maybe even dunked it. Jerome turned to see but it was too late to tell what happened. He looked quickly at Cincy, walking beside him in a random, shuffling, distracted sort of way—suddenly, she moved up next to him so that their hips touched. "Hey, you wanna date me or what?" she said.

"Let's see."

"Give me some drugs and I'll give you half price, OK?"

He nodded and mumbled.

"You definitely gonna get me high, right?"

"Yes."

"Lookit, Jerome, stop being so sad about that little bitch, OK? Date me instead. It will serve her right for being late."

"Her name is Abby and I'd appreciate . . ."

"Oh, Abby! I know Abby. *Everyone* knows Abby. They call her Abby Road 'cause so many men have traveled on her."

He stopped walking and looked hard at her and for the first time Cincy looked a little frightened.

"Hey, I'm just kidding. I don't know no Abby. Calm down. Are you like, in love with her or something?"

"She isn't my girlfriend."

"But you'd like her to be. So you like 'em young, huh? Well I'm still young. I'm young enough for you, ain't I?"

"Yes, you're young."

"So what's so special about this Abby?"

"The way we talked," he said. "We could talk about anything. People don't know how to talk anymore."

"I can talk, too. You can tell me anything—believe me, I've heard everything."

"OK. What do you think about what I just said? What are your thoughts about it?"

He snuck another look at her and was surprised to see a serious expression in her eyes.

"I think sometimes people talk too much and sometimes not enough."

"Abby was kind. She knew when to talk and when to listen."

"What about me, for Christ's sake? Don't you think I'm kind? God, you're making me feel like I should die or something. My father used to do the same thing to me, that's probably why I ran away from home."

"I'm not trying to make you feel bad. I just don't know you very well."

"Well, don't you think I'm kind so far?"

"Yes, you're being nice," he said softly, keeping his head away from her because he was lying. He didn't like the way she kept discrediting Abby, and that joke about her was unforgivable. Besides, Cincy was a whore and whores only cared about money and drugs, in no particular order. Whores could be truly frightening, although some could be as easy to control as clay.

"Here's my street," he said, "and there's my building."

"Oh," she said. "It's like a duplex."

"Yuh, but I have both apartments."

"No shit. I guess you do have some serious bucks, then."

"My apartments are all that's in the house," he said, as he took out the keys and began opening the different locks. Cincy counted four of them. When she stepped into his apartment she thought how big it was and then how relatively empty, as if it were a concert hall or some kind of strange museum. There were just a couple of tables, a few chairs, and a small sofa. It would be a weird place to get high.

"You said you wanted a beer."

"Yuh, for starters."

He walked across the floor making a kind of echo as he moved because it was so empty. The kitchen was at the far end of the floor.

"Sit down on the sofa, why don't you," he said rather loudly. She noticed a little table beside the sofa where there was a photograph of a gray-haired woman with penetrating eyes. He returned with two glasses, a can of Heineken, and some coasters. When he sat down next to her she said, "Who's in the picture?"

"It's my mother. I have a very clear picture of Abby in my mind so I don't need to look at a photograph of her but I sometimes forget what my mother looks like, which is . . . disturbing . . . so I keep a photograph of her here."

She took a long drink and stared at him.

"I'll never forget what my mother looks like."

"Well, that's healthy of you," he said, paying her back, he thought.

She didn't appear to notice. Instead, she took a big swallow of her drink, and followed that with several smaller swallows. He didn't have high hopes for her intelligence, although he couldn't be too sure since meanness and intelligence often overlapped.

"I think if we remember what someone looks like it's 'cause we love them in some way," she said.

"I mostly remember what my mother looks like, by the way, it's just that sometimes I . . ."

"What I say has got to be true or we wouldn't remember anyone, right? Even animals got to remember some things, right?"

He stared at her without saying anything, thinking that she wasn't a frightening whore after all. He could even picture her on the first floor and maybe one day soon on the second.

"Don't that make sense, don't that make great sense? See, I told you I was smart."

"Sure, that's why we keep pictures of people," Jerome said. "That's why we write diaries and books. Almost everything in people's apartments is a way to remember. See, if only I had taken . . . a photograph of Abby I wouldn't be feeling this . . . terrible frustration."

"You can take a photograph of me. I could make myself look like her if you'd tell me more of what she looked like. I could act like her too if you told me what she acted like. I'm very good at acting. My plan is, a little down the road, to become an actress."

"Really?" he said, with a tinge of sarcasm.

"Yuh, really. I just need to change some things in my life. You know, I just need a chance."

He smiled. For the first time since he'd come to the park and saw that Abby was missing he felt a lightness in his head. It was like coming out of a thick woods into a clearing.

"See, I'm not really that much of a hooker. I just don't have a home right now so sometimes I've got to do things to get a place to stay. But if I could get a place where I could stay then I could study and, like, become an actress, and then one day you could brag about knowing me. Hey, what did you put in this beer, huh? Jesus Christ!" she said, laughing for a second, as if in disbelief.

"You said you wanted to get high."

"You sure did keep your promise. Wow . . . Hey, if you still wanna date me, now would be a great time," she said, opening her legs suggestively.

"Is that why you didn't take money from me for a cab? 'Cause you have no place to go to?"

"Yuh," she said, looking down at the floor and figuring out something about him. "See, if you was to let me stay here on one of your floors, even just for a while, you could make me look like Abby . . . if you wanted to, and then you wouldn't miss her so much."

"Please don't say her name anymore."

"OK. I could look like her though and you could teach me how to act like her and then you wouldn't have really lost her. So, what do you think?"

He had leaned back against the sofa. Cincy imagined he was deep in thought. It seemed like months passed before he spoke.

"I got a question for you, are you ready? It's kind of a riddle. Which one of these do you pick? Happy Birthday, the Snowman, or Cary Grant?"

"Who's Cary Grant?"

"No questions, just pick one."

"OK. Happy Birthday. I pick Happy Birthday."

"All right. So what do you want for your birthday?"

"I wanna stay here . . . just for a little while."

"Fine. Wish granted."

"Really? Thanks Jerome. That's really sweet of you. Jerry, can I call you that? What's your upstairs like, can I see it?"

"Later . . . maybe."

"Shit, what've you got up there, a meth lab or something?"

"Don't ask so many questions. Abby wouldn't."

"OK, sorry."

"Abby would just enjoy the moment and not worry about the future or the past. I, myself, have never been able to do that, but she could."

"Take a drink of what you gave me and that might do it."

But he didn't take it. Instead he stayed close to her during her high, sitting upright on the sofa and even standing when she started running around the room dancing and laughing and saying, "This is heaven, this is paradise." That part of it lasted almost an hour, followed by a long silent period as she lay on the sofa staring at the ceiling, which she thought was an ocean at first but later thought was a slow-moving, silent lake. He gave her a kaleidoscope then so she could see "what a sunrise in heaven" looks like, and she spent a long time looking through it.

When she began to come down a little he put in a video by Eric Carle, who made lovely movies for children. This video had four short films in it—"The Very Hungry Caterpillar," "Papa, Please Get the Moon for Me," "The Mixed-up Chameleon," and the most overtly psychedelic of the lot, "I See a Song."

Cincy, who had been talking very rapidly, got quiet while she watched. "That's so awesome," she said, with tears filling her eyes. Then she asked if she could watch it again. He brought in a bowl of popcorn, an apple, and a can of beer for her, figuring she must be hungry, and watched her, thinking that he would like to see her look like Abby—that they were close enough in age and size that it was possible. Already in his mind's eye he was picturing the women's clothing store near him where he could buy her jeans and a green top and then the eye-wear store, where he could buy her blue or green contact lenses, though it would be hard to get blue/green. Her hair would have to be lightened a bit and rearranged so she'd have bangs in front and a ponytail in back. It would take work but was doable.

He could see that she was slowly coming down and that the food and beer were making her tired.

"I've had a really great day," she said.

"Good, I'm glad. I'm going to leave a key to this apartment next to the picture of my mother. It's for you and you alone to use. Don't bring anyone else over under any circumstances, OK? If you need something ask me for it, but don't bring anyone over to do drugs or anything else. That's my one rule, all right?"

"For sure, definitely."

He wasn't surprised when halfway through her third viewing of the movie she fell asleep on the sofa. He too was tired and soon went upstairs to the top floor, where his bedroom was, and fell asleep in his bed.

She must have slept a very long time, although she had her clothes on and spent the whole night on his smallish sofa. When she woke up there were marks on her forearm from the sofa as if it had tattooed her. Jerome was gone. She called his name, even walked up the flight of stairs to the second floor (where the door was padlocked), but he didn't answer.

She went back to the living room and turned on the TV. After a couple of shows she heard the first-floor locks opening one by one. When he walked in he was carrying three shopping bags full of clothes.

. . . .

He was a hard one to figure, a tough nut to crack. There were times when he seemed completely immersed in describing how Abby looked and spoke, moments, especially after she finally got the contacts to hold and her hairstyle right, when he was almost ecstatic, but then he would lose interest and a minute or so later disappear upstairs.

He had not made any pass at her, he didn't seem interested, though he continued to feed her both food and drugs and was treating her well enough. She was glad not to have to go to the park looking for tricks and crank. Whatever it was he was giving her (he said it was a special kind of organic mescaline) was working, though she was beginning to get restless even as she was also starting to feel at home. For one thing she hadn't left the house except for one short walk with him to a deli where they bought beer. For another, she still didn't have a dime to her name. She had been in his house for a week and still not done any work. The next time she saw him she said, "I'm thinking that I need to work."

"By working you mean hooking, right?"

"You got any other ideas how I can make my own money? I don't have no degrees from anywhere, you know. It's not like I got a masters from Harvard."

"What do you need money for exactly? Anything you need that you're not getting?"

"I just feel better with some cash in my pocket."

"Here," he said, taking two one hundred dollar bills from his pocket and half tossing them onto her little table by the sofa. "Will that hold you for a while?"

She couldn't help looking at them for a second to be sure they were real then said, "Thanks Jerry, thanks a lot."

He turned away, walking toward the opposite end of the long living room. Then he opened the refrigerator and began drinking a beer.

The next day he took several photographs of her dressed as Abby. He did it in a serious, businesslike way that disappointed her. What was the point of it, after all, if he didn't have fun? Then he left her alone for the rest of the afternoon, probably to look for Abby again in the park.

When he returned it was early evening (she'd done nothing but watch TV) yet he walked by her as if she were a tree or a rock, barely saying hello. This time she ran after him, catching up to him while he was opening the locks on the second floor. She still hadn't seen his apartment, which only added to her frustration.

"Don't you talk to me anymore?" she said from the foot of the stairs. She started up the stairs and he seemed to freeze, his face whitening as if bleach had been added to it.

"You left me alone all day, you know. Can't you talk to me before you leave me alone all night?"

He looked at her darkly—she was openly staring at his keys.

"What did you want to talk about?"

"I see you're about to go into your little world. Am I ever gonna see it?"

"Why is that so important to you?"

She shrugged. " I just wanna know about you. I mean we're living in the same house, ain't we?"

He nodded, as if considering the rationality of her request.

"When I'm dying can you carry me upstairs and show it to me then?"

"That depends," he said, in his deadpan voice. He never seemed to find anything she said funny, which also reminded her of her father.

"Oh yuh, what's it depend on?"

"How you die. The way you die."

"Well, I can't tell that so . . ."

"On the contrary, I think you can. I think if we look at it closely enough, everyone chooses the way they die. Think about it."

"Yuh, OK, I will." He was always speaking to her in riddles. It was like being pestered by a low-grade mosquito. "Lookit, Jerry, can you come downstairs in a little while and just watch TV with me or something?"

She expected the worst but he surprised her by saying he'd join her in a few minutes. Then she got an idea. She had some crushed powder from a sleeping pill in a little zip-lock bag deep in her skirt pocket—the only clothes she'd worn all week except for the Abby clothes he'd bought her. She decided she'd have his Heineken waiting for him but would add the powder (which was both colorless and odorless) to his drink. She thought if he loosened up maybe he'd have sex with her and if they had sex he'd let her stay indefinitely, maybe even forever. In the unlikely event that he'd realized what happened and was angry she could claim she gave him her drink by mistake. After all, she was the one always using his drugs and she'd never pressed him to take anything before. Why would he suspect her?

It was odd watching him drink and waiting for signs of the drug to show. She unbuttoned her shirt and spread her legs apart to try to speed up the process but his face—vacant and rigid—was glued to the TV, where one of those dumb WB girl shows was on. Why couldn't he look at her the way he was staring at those stupid actresses?

"You like TV a lot?" she asked him.

"I have measured out my life in TV shows." Another riddle. It was typical. She drank from her own beer, watching him intermittently. Every now and then she had a john who couldn't get it up, but at least they made an effort. He'd never even tried with her—never showed any interest at all, not even when she dressed up like Abby. And it wasn't like he was *that* old, either. Well, at least he could talk to her. The way it was going she barely felt she existed.

"Jerry?"

"Yuh."

"Before you got your money what did you used to do?"

"Sold things."

"What'd you sell?"

"Does it matter? Everybody sells things except children, some children at least. That's what working is. It made me angry but I had to do it."

She couldn't think of anything to say. He had a way of killing the topics she brought up—like shooting snakes right in their tracks.

"Jerry?"

"Yuh?"

"You know that riddle you asked me the first day I came here about Cary Grant."

"What about it?"

"What if I had picked the Snowman? What would have happened to me?"

"Aren't you happy with what you picked, with Happy Birthday?"

"Yuh, sure, but what if I'd picked the Snowman?"

"You don't need to know that. Be glad for what you did pick, and don't worry about what you didn't."

Again, he had shut her off, but at least he said it in a nice voice. She hated it when an angry edge crept into it. Maybe the drug was starting to work now and was making him mellower.

"Jerry?"

"Yuh."

"You still interested in screwing girls?"

He looked away from her with a kind of stricken expression on his face.

"What kind of question is that?"

"OK, put it this way—you interested in doing me or not?"

He turned his head to face her but it was as if he were looking past her.

"You've done things for me already, and you're gonna do more . . . why do you ask?"

"I been here a week and you ain't even tried to touch me. It makes me kind of nervous—like you don't like me."

He nodded slowly. When he spoke now it was slower too. "Get in your clothes (which meant the Abby clothes) and I'll give you something to do. Change your hair and put in your eyes too."

She got up from the sofa, glad that something was finally going to happen. Of course it would have been nice to be a little more romantic and spontaneous—which was what she had hoped for. It would have been nice, too, not to have to look like *her*—she thought as she put in the contacts, then started rearranging her hair. But at least they were going to have some kind of sex—probably her sucking him somewhere, she guessed, but still it was a beginning.

He was a mysterious one with lots of secrets and she couldn't really expect to solve the mystery right away, though she was dying to solve it, dying to know everything about him because he'd been kinder to her already than any man ever had. Why couldn't she have had a father like that? Somehow things got mixed up in life. Jerry took care of her and gave her a peaceful home and her father criticized her all the time and made her have sex with him till she finally left home.

She checked her bangs and lipstick in the mirror and then returned to the sofa, where she saw him passed out with his mouth open, snoring slightly. He looked tender and young somehow and she knew she'd do anything for him if he wanted. She just had to be patient and have faith and it would eventually happen. Then she saw something gold sticking out of his pocket. It was the keys to his floor!

It was odd to have something you wanted in this world work out. It was almost paralyzing. Even his snoring seemed calculated to reassure her about how deeply he was sleeping.

The keys were bunched up and already half out of his pocket. Since she had done a fair amount of pocket picking in her life it was one of the simplest lifts she'd ever done. One touch and they were hers. Maybe he'd turned away from her body—though she'd see about that—she was far from giving up—but at least she'd finally get to see that other world he had on that forbidden second floor.

She walked lightly on her tiptoes toward the stairs. The wood seemed to be cooperating too, as if it were a co-conspirator, and there was scarcely a creak while she moved. She had lived only a little more than a week with him but it felt like much longer—and sometimes as if she'd always lived there. That's why the reaction of the wood didn't surprise her—it was as if she'd mastered it, knowing just where to step to move as quietly as possible up the staircase. It was the same confidence she felt about eventually having sex with him. Once they started she felt sure she would know what he wanted and how to do it. She would master his body like she did the stairs—that was her profession, after all.

The locks did give her a little trouble but only a little. There were four of them that had to be matched with the few keys. But she'd watched him do it a couple of times and it wasn't really difficult. The important thing was she made very little noise doing it. A couple of minutes later the door gave and she stepped into his home.

The first thing she saw was a whiteness that matched the white Abby dress she'd changed into. For a few seconds it was empty and pure like the downstairs. She took a couple of more steps into the living room until she became aware of a strong smell in the air—rancid and almost overpowering. Then she turned into his bedroom and saw something horrifying in a kind of flash. Instantly her eyes blinked shut and wouldn't open again until she'd backed away from the place where she saw it or thought she saw it. Didn't really open her eyes—though her heart was beating so fast she thought *it* was opening—until she redid the locks.

It had been a flash, like lightning, and who can see anything for sure when lightning explodes in front of them, she thought, as she ran down the stairs. By the time she saw him still asleep on the sofa she was sure that she hadn't really seen anything, certainly nothing identifiable, that it was probably just a vision or an inner fear of hers she momentarily projected onto the world. People could do that, especially addicts. She'd seen it before. She couldn't be certain, but thought maybe that's what happened to her.

She sat down next to him—he was still snoring—and lightly touched his hair and then his sleeping shoulders. The one thing she knew was she had a home at last and that she never had to see the second floor, there was no reason to, since she had her own home on the first. A home that he'd given her. When she closed her eyes it was as if the second floor didn't even exist.

VIVIAN AND SID
BREAK UP

"Is this a bad time?"

"No, it's all right, Sid, it's fine."

The last three weeks Sid had called Vivian every day, sometimes more than once and never at the same time, making her worry that eventually he would call at such a bad time she'd have to tell him to try back later, which she's sure he'd take in the worst possible way.

"Because if it's not, I could call back."

"No, Sid, it's OK. It really is fine."

Each time he phoned, Vivian couldn't help picturing where he was and what he was wearing. This time she imagined him in a La-Z-Boy, although she didn't remember if there were any in his brother's apartment, cradling the cordless phone against his white tee shirt (the one with two nickel-sized holes under the left arm) watching the TV on mute.

"You have to admit that since you broke up with me I've been very restrained, considering it's me this happened to."

"Yes, you've been considerate and, once again, I didn't break up with you."

"Not break up with me? What do you call it then—a leave of absence?"

"Sid, I told you I basically just needed some time apart to think. I mean I know it's upsetting, it is for me too, but . . ."

"You used to be able to think while we were together . . ."

"Not always that well," she said, trying not to sound sarcastic.

"I thought you were thinking just fine—you published books, you got a full professorship, that's more than I ever did."

"It's not that kind of thinking, Sid, that I'm talking about."

"What then? What kind of thinking is it?"

"Thinking about the future, about what I want. It's life thinking."

"Life thinking?"

"OK, admittedly a silly phrase. I mean evaluating my life and what I want in it while I'm still young enough to do something about it. You know I'm fifty-one now, not exactly a child."

"May I remind you that I'm six years older than you, my beauty queen. And what are you evaluating? You've been with me for thirteen or fourteen years. Don't you know what I'm like, already? What don't you know about me by now? You know I'm not the smartest man on earth and certainly not the richest or tallest. That I'm basically an aging, bony little paranoid nutcase Jew who thanked his lucky stars every night that he had you."

She pictured the hurt expression in his eyes, like a child feeling himself wronged. At barely five foot four, Sidney was sensitive about his height, as he was about his age, his expanding bald spot, his religion, his inability to get promoted at her college, his love of television, and just about anything having to do with their sex life.

"I don't hear you answering me, Viv. I'm not getting any younger here waiting for an answer."

"I don't know what else to say, Sid. I've been saying the same thing to you every day. It seems like we're talking in circles."

"I could use a little reassurance."

"Reassurance?"

"Yes, if you still say, you haven't broken up with me, yet. If that's really true. Although I have to say, when I see my bed empty every night it definitely feels like you've left."

"I've left you temporarily so I can think."

"Again, with the thinking. Must life always be so complicated?"

"Sid, I love you, OK?"

"Finally you say the magic words, or some of them."

"I tell you that every time you call, don't I?"

"It doesn't mean you'll feel it by the time the next call comes. It could die in between calls."

Vivian laughed. He was speaking in his little-boy mode, one of his most charming she had to admit, in part because it was so unaffected.

"It's not a balloon Sid, that's suddenly going to break."

"It's hard not to feel that way when I'm away from you for so long, and when I feel like you're deliberating like a judge about what to finally do with me . . ."

"With *us*."

"Yes, the almighty future."

"Is it unreasonable to think about what's ahead of us?"

"I don't understand. Last year you were hung up about the past. You were afraid that you were losing too many memories, that you were inventing your past because you couldn't really remember it."

"That was two years ago, Sid, not one."

"Again, I'm wrong. But at least we know you still have a good, functioning memory."

Vivian forced a polite laugh but began to feel alarmed. Whenever Sid started to be sarcastic it was often a sign of worse things to come.

"So, my beauty queen, I've been with you when you've been hung up about the past and now when you're hung up about the future. What I want to know is when are you going to get hung up about me in the present?"

"Sid, do you ever wonder why we never got married?" She suddenly blurted, surprising herself as much as him by her remark.

"This we have also talked about a few thousand times."

"Yes, we've talked about it, but if we were so right for each other did you ever wonder why it didn't happen?"

"You were traumatized by your marriage, I was traumatized by mine. How's that for starters?"

"Sure, that could explain why we postponed it the first few years. But what about, say, the last ten years?"

"I thought we were happy so why rock the boat? But if that's what this is about, if that's what you're angry about there's an easy enough solution . . ."

"I'm not angry, and certainly not about that," she said, although she did feel an unmistakable tension throughout her body.

"You're not angry but you're managing to yell at me pretty well."

"I'm sorry . . . I wasn't aware. You know I raise my voice the way other people raise their eyebrows. Look Sid, do you remember that novel I told you about, *The Unbearable Lightness of Being?*

"Ah, I knew there had to be a book behind this."

"Please don't be sarcastic. It doesn't become you."

"No, it's just that you turn to books whenever you have a crisis the way other people turn to therapists and, just like the therapists, sometimes these books are what actually create the crisis."

"That's completely unfair."

"Honestly, Vivian, I liked it more when we were living in Brookline. There at least there were a few acres that were book free. But since we moved to Harvard Square, the bookstore capital of the universe, a lot more crises have been popping up."

"Well, you're in Brookline now so that should make you happy," she said, immediately regretting her remark.

"I'm in Brookline 'cause my brother's letting me stay with him for a while only because he's got the space for me since his divorce. I'm not exactly Donald Trump that I can just check into a Cambridge hotel because you've suddenly decided that you're sick of me."

"I'm sorry. That was mean of me. Can you accept my apology?"

"Apology accepted," Sid said tersely.

"Getting back to the book . . ."

"The Being Unbearable book?"

"*The Unbearable Lightness of Being.* There's an interesting idea in it, actually the title kind of expresses it—that life is unbearably light because we can only do everything once. Life isn't a dress rehearsal, but a final performance that happens only once."

"And . . . so?"

"So everything we decide to do with ourselves and other people is in one sense eternal because it can't be undone, is our irreversible fate because . . ."

"So it all boils down to you haven't decided if I'm good enough for you yet. You haven't decided if you want to spend the rest of your life with me or not."

"Jesus Christ!" she hissed into the phone with her jaw clenched in that embarrassingly masculine way it always did when she was angry. "You're not listening to a thing I say."

"What do you want me to say Viv, what do you want me to do?"

"Do whatever you want. Use this time to find out what you want," she said, still more angrily than she wanted to.

"I want you."

"You're just used to me. Why don't you date other people?"

"What?"

"Yes, date other women. Your brother, David, knows lots of women. Maybe he could fix you up with one who's better suited for you than me."

"Are you serious? Are you being serious or are you altogether me-shuga?"

"No, I'm speaking to you as a friend."

"I don't want you as a friend. Friends don't make love."

"Maybe we need to be friends for a little while. Put our fears away and be friends."

"My fear right now is that you don't want me any more."

"And my fear is that you only want me out of habit, out of fear of anything different happening in your life. It's like your religion is 'Don't Rock the Boat' and that's why we never . . . that's why we're in this rut we're in and that's why I want you to see other women so you can realize who I am; see the differences between people and then really be able to choose who you want."

"Vivian, you're a human being, not a habit."

"I'm not a very happy human being these days, however," she said, wishing she didn't sound so self-pitying but persisting anyway. "That's why I need to be alone right now."

"And are you also going to 'grow' as well by going out with other men?"

"Sid, I already said I needed to be alone. Alone means alone, as in no other men."

At last there was a silence. She could hear him breathing, feel him thinking, and she took the opportunity to initiate the mutual reassurances with which their conversations usually ended, though this time she felt that nothing had really ended at all.

Then she hung up and screamed into her empty bedroom, almost seeing the surprising noise she produced fill each corner of her room like a giant wave from the ocean, the kind one never got at Cape Cod but had to travel to Atlantic City to see. It was still only 9 P.M. and she thought she might work out at the gym she'd just joined—something else Sid frowned upon, probably because it threatened him. She thought if she hustled she could have an hour workout and still get a good night's sleep, but she ended up organizing some papers that were starting to congregate on her office desk.

Later, in bed, feeling defeated by all the channels on her TV, she'd wondered if she meant what she'd said to Sid about dating other women and why she'd suddenly said it at all. Because Sid was always the overtly insecure one in the relationship, she usually acted more self-confident and what she said was certainly, at face value, a supreme expression of self-confidence. But didn't it also contain an element of cruelty, the awareness of which was making it difficult for her to fall asleep? What if *he* had said that to her—which, of course, would never happen, he wouldn't risk it—but what if he had? She would be shocked, perhaps laugh at first because she'd never doubted his fidelity at any point in their long relationship (it was he who, erroneously, sometimes doubted her). But still, sooner rather than later, such an invitation would hurt her. Ah, how she hated hurting Sid and rarely tried to even when she was angry, so why had she said it to guileless, endlessly sweet, touchingly funny Sid, the only person besides her father (who died ten years ago) who could bring tears to her eyes just by thinking about him for a few seconds?

All her life, as she remembered it, she'd essentially tried to please people and not rock the boat herself. It began with trying to please her parents, especially her father. She was always the straight-A student who never got in trouble but seethed with secret contempt for her school. Later, when she became a teacher, also in large part to please her father, she was successful and was even the department head for seven years, which ultimately allowed her to push through Sid's tenure. Still, she never lost her sense of absurdity about the university, society in general, and beyond that, the proposition of life itself.

She'd wanted to be a novelist but hadn't dared. Instead, she'd written scholarly books and articles on Jane Austen and the Brontës. She had married the first time—a ridiculous, immediately ill-fated marriage—mostly to please her parents as well. When that ended and she met Sid, she hadn't dared to suggest having children with him when he was in his mid-forties because she felt he didn't want them, only to realize later that he secretly, if ambivalently, did.

Occasionally, however, she *would* disturb the status quo with an outrageous remark or small impulsive act—things that Sid would never do. She supposed that when she urged him to date, almost insisting on it, she was rocking the boat again, but this time it was Sid who would possibly fall out and have to sink or swim.

She looked at her clock on top of the TV. It was too late to phone tonight but she would definitely call him early tomorrow.

• • • • • • • • • •

Strange to get a call from someone every day for three weeks, someone you'd lived with for almost thirteen years, and then not be able to get them on the telephone. Of course she'd awakened later than she'd planned so it was understandable, if surprising, that Sid was already out. It was Saturday and she decided to walk to Weidner to do research, then eat lunch someplace in Harvard Square.

But, in the library, she had trouble concentrating and found herself thinking about Sid, remembering their vacations in Cape Cod and their unlikely trip to Hawaii, unlikely (though it turned out so well) because of his fear of spending money. She thought she might ask him to join her for lunch, then decided one call from her was enough for a morning, that she should wait for him to call her.

As she suspected, when she returned to her apartment, she had a message from him.

"Hi Viv, it's Sid. I thought I'd let you know that I'm shopping with my brother this morning. I guess he's also sick of looking at me and wants me to get some kind of makeover. Ha ha. Oh, and by the way, I'm following your orders and have a blind date for tonight with someone my brother fixed me up with, like you suggested. You see how flexible I'm being? I'm still dreaming of you every night, hoping to see you the sooner the better, of course. Well . . . so long."

This was quite a development! Vivian was so nonplussed that she nearly sat on her kitten. Her first impulse was to wonder if it was true. How could someone get a date Saturday for that same Saturday night? Except that Sid didn't lie. He was the only person she knew (now that her father had died) who didn't. He didn't even manipulate people—wouldn't know how—one of the reasons he'd never become a full professor. Of course, she had only herself to blame for all this. She walked into the bathroom and wasn't surprised to see tears welling up in her large blue eyes. Looking down at the glass counter she saw the hair rinse she used to keep herself a brunette. In the cabinet were her blush, her skin cream, mascara, and other makeup, but what was the point of it all if she couldn't keep Sid?

She returned to their bedroom and listened to his message again. What was so galling was the sheer pride he couldn't help revealing so baldly when he announced he had a date, as if he were a twelve-year-old telling his mother he'd won a prize at the school science fair. She could see his little black eyes sparkling with pleasure, the self-congratulating smile out on his face as plain as a red shirt on a clothesline. The man was incapable of dissimulation (it was a big part of what she loved about him, damn it), whereas she dissimulated without even realizing it as if it were so deeply a part of her nature (Sid would say of women's nature) she couldn't help it and wound up fooling herself too, at least for a little while.

Well, she couldn't tell him not to go now. To reverse herself would play into every stereotype Sid believed about her in particular and women in general. The thought of that was enough to bring her tears back and make her curse herself for her foolish pride again, or whatever it was.

. . . .

At best, Sidney thought, looking in the mirror could make you happy for a few seconds, but the older you got the fewer those seconds became. And

when he felt anxious, as he did now, trimming his moustache and combing his hair before his blind date, which virtually screamed "unmitigated
disaster" at him, it was better to look as little as possible. How had this
happened to him? It had begun with Vivian's virtual demand that he date
other women, of course, and then continued when he made the mistake
of confiding about it to his younger brother, David, who had a habit of
making him feel worse when he wanted reassurance, instead of better.
Why was Viv telling him to date, he'd asked David, did she just want to
get rid of him?

"I don't know, God forbid. That's why I smell a rat," David had said.

"David, you're scaring me already."

"That I don't mean to do. Look Sid, calm down. When it comes to
women no one's an expert. I don't really know what she's thinking. You
say she's a straightforward person."

"I always thought so."

"So take what she says at face value. Maybe it's true."

Then there was a transition and David began trying to convince him
that he should go out and that he knew just the person for him, namely,
his girlfriend Paula's best friend, Phyllis. The next thing Sid knew, he'd
gone from seeking reassurance about Vivian, who he'd been with for thirteen years, to seeking reassurance about a woman he'd never even met.

"So this Phyllis is a friend of your girlfriend, right, and I take it 'a nice
Jewish girl,'" Sid had said a little sarcastically, since David had never fully
approved of Viv being a shiksa.

"She's Jewish, she's nice, and nice looking too, and believe me still hot
to trot."

Sidney had waved an arm dismissively. "David, what are you saying?
I'm not interested."

"Keep an open mind," David had said. "I know that's the hardest thing
to do after a divorce."

"Divorce? David, we were never married."

"Sorry. I meant separated. It was the hardest thing for me to do after
my divorce. But these last six months I've been having a very good time
with Paula so all I'm saying is keep an open mind. OK?"

If David had talked any more and made him any more nervous his mind would be closed forever in a psycho ward . . . Well, at least he was done with his mirror, Sid thought, after one last glance at his moustache and hair. He left the bathroom, checked his fly, checked his keys, credit cards, and cash in his wallet, checked the windows, heat, and water faucets, and then, address in hand, finally felt able to face the city, where his date was also waiting blindly for him.

. . . .

She had been lying in her bubble bath for five minutes now without moving, still reviewing her recent phone call with Paula.

"That's so *you*, Phyllis," Paula had said with conviction. Paula was one of those people who always seemed to be summing her up, Phyllis thought, always telling her what she was but she was invariably wrong or else right in the most minute of ways, as if she'd correctly identified her toes underwater without seeing the rest of her looming above.

"What is? What's so like me?" Phyllis had said.

"Changing your mind at the last minute."

"This whole date thing is at the last minute."

"All the more reason to want me and David along, I would've thought, we'd make it less awkward for both of you. He's Sidney's brother for God's sake and I'm like your sister, aren't I?" Paula had said, vastly overrating her importance in her life, as she often did. But Phyllis had let the remark go and instead changed the subject.

"So, this Sidney, is he a nice man?"

"He's David's brother and David's crazy about him."

"But do you think he's nice?"

"Yes, he's a nice man. He's a professor."

A professor, then what would she talk about, Phyllis had said laughing, making fun of herself, really, but why did she do that so much when she knew she was intelligent enough to date a professor or anyone else, for that matter.

"Don't worry, he's not an intellectual," Paula had said, meaning to reassure her but actually hurting her in the process. "He's different. He's funny. He teaches English or Comparative Lit, something like that—but you'd never know it."

"And he's decent looking, I'm afraid to ask?"

"He's adorable."

"Not fat or bald?"

"He's skinny and still has some hair and a cute mustache. He's a little short, but not too bad. You see him, you want to cuddle him and more."

"OK Paula, now I *really* want to be alone with him," she'd said, then added that Paula should stay home and have a private party with David, that David would love that.

Paula laughed. "You're right about that. You can't imagine how much. I'll bet Sidney will be the same way."

"Which leads me to my last question," she'd said. "I'm going to take a bath soon and I thought about shaving myself. What do you think?"

"You mean, . . . down there?"

"Bingo. You think Sidney is the type who'd like it?"

"All men like it, but he wouldn't be finding out for a while, would he?"

"You never know what can happen, am I right? I mean if everything goes perfect with this nutty professor, who knows?"

She had a smile on her face now, a little surprised at how bluntly she'd spoken as she finally began to wash herself. She'd sounded so light and confident on the phone talking to Paula, and that was the way to feel, wasn't it? But, now, ten minutes later, she felt oddly ridiculous and isolated and had to put the facecloth down.

How many times had she done this—wash herself alone—over the years? It seemed she could still remember her first unsupervised bath when she was six or seven, and now thousands of baths later she was still doing it—washing her skin and later her clothes and dishes. It all ran together, this endless seesaw of washing and drying, as if it were half of life. But what exactly was the point of this perpetual quest to clean one's self and one's things? It was as if the point of it had drowned long ago in the water while the activity went on and on.

She washed another five minutes before getting out of the tub and drying herself, then standing before her mirror naked with shaving cream in one hand and a razor in the other. Was she really going to do this, which meant was she really going to let there be a chance that this little professor could see it? Here she was, forty-eight years old, still not knowing why she did or didn't do things. Hadn't she just retired a washcloth and now she stood in front of her bathroom mirror with a razor trying to decide if she should make herself look like a little girl or not? Maybe that was the point, what she and the men whom it aroused liked so much. Maybe it was all about one more glimpse of bold, pristine, unimaginable youth? How did that song go—"Get back to where you once belonged?"

Why was she having these strange thoughts again? It seemed she often had them before blind dates. Why not just shave, and with a few careful strokes be done with it and end this unsettling line of thought. What did she have to lose?

And so she concentrated the way she hadn't since she left art school once and for all in her early twenties, the way she only did now when she washed and shaved and cleaned for men—husbands or bosses or fix-ups. It all ran together after a while. And when she was done and had put on her Victoria's Secret underwear, she decided to reward herself with a strong gin martini.

. . . .

This is the height of ridiculousness, Sidney thought, to be going on a date he didn't want to go on—his mind flooded every moment with memories of Viv—and at the same time, to be worried about what he should do, how he should behave, to be nervous as a schoolboy. But the fact was the last time he'd gone on a first date with a woman was with Vivian thirteen or fourteen years ago, he couldn't be sure which. He had been a different person then, with a full head of black hair. Now it was almost embarrassing to appear at a strange woman's door (what an ingenious punishment Viv had contrived for him) and not even knowing with *what* to appear. Flowers? Candy? Did men still bring women these things? He should have asked David. He didn't want to be impolite or cheap (especially since he knew he *was* on the frugal side), but he didn't want to scare the woman either. He decided on a small spring bouquet to match the season, though it was a typically cold April night in Boston.

Another thing was on his mind, as he finally found her apartment on Charles Street and rang the buzzer. Why had she decided against the double date? It would have all gone so much easier with David and Paula along to be the star conversationalists. He could have faded into the background imperceptibly enough and in two and a half hours—about the length of an evening at the movies—the torture would be over. What had made this woman prefer to meet a stranger one on one? Did she have something against David perhaps? Or was she one of those who didn't talk well even in a small group? He, himself, had always preferred to dine alone with Viv or, when he had to see other people, to be alone with them too. Otherwise, he felt he had to divide himself up emotionally and that was never pleasant.

He heard the door ring, still not even her voice, though perhaps it was the fault of the intercom, and the next thing he knew he was riding up an elevator, clutching his flowers, feeling anxious and sad and apologetic for even taking this poor woman's time when he was totally consumed with Vivian.

Phyllis greeted him at the door very warmly, as if he were a close relative, smiling so much he couldn't get a good view of her face.

"Hi, come in. Sit down. Have a drink. Thank you so much for the beautiful flowers," she'd said to him in a rush before he could barely say hello back.

Sidney walked in a few steps. "You're place is nice," he said, sounding positively solemn by comparison, and she smiled even harder, acting as if she'd received the greatest compliment of her life.

The fact was he could barely focus on her apartment. He only knew he was in a place that wasn't his and was eager to get out of it, to start the exit process of the evening that would have to begin at a restaurant more expensive than the ones he normally ate at with Viv.

But Phyllis had other ideas. After finally getting him to sit down and accept a glass of water, she said, "Do you mind if we just talk for a while?"

"Of course not," he said, still unable to make eye contact with her. He did notice she was wearing a pink, lacy-looking skirt that had risen higher when she sat on the sofa next to him. She had nice legs and was about his height—probably three inches shorter than Vivian, so at least she wouldn't be too embarrassed walking into a restaurant with him.

After ten minutes of chitchat, nine minutes of which emanated from her, he said, "I came up with the names of three restaurants for tonight."

"I'm not *that* hungry," Phyllis joked.

"Ha ha! Good one. I only ask you to pick one and then perhaps I can cancel the other two reservations that I already made."

"I have a better idea. Why don't you let me fix you something here?"

"Oh no, I couldn't."

"No, really, I'd enjoy that."

"No, no, out of the question."

"But I'd prefer it, really, I insist."

"No, I couldn't let you do that," he said, trying to look and sound serious, though he would appreciate saving the sixty to eighty dollars and somehow would also feel less exposed in this woman's apartment than in a restaurant with all its chattering witnesses.

"But I've already made a salad and desert. Do you like chicken?"

"Sure, of course, but . . ."

"Then I can just heat it up. Come on Sidney, come into the kitchen and keep me company while I cook."

"OK, if this is what you want. Thank you," he added.

For a while it was diverting to watch her prepare their meal, but the smell of chicken cooking reminded him of times he'd spent in the kitchen with Viv watching and sometimes even helping her cook and the pain nearly leveled him. Then, suddenly, Phyllis staggered herself, clutching onto the counter to regain her balance.

"Are you OK?" Sid said.

"Yes. I guess I just lost my step."

He nodded. She had an odd way of talking. Everything about her seemed odd, as if her entire being were slightly out of focus. He didn't want to stay in the kitchen any longer but could hardly tell her that now, so asked if he could use the bathroom. He figured that there he could at least collect himself and deal with this latest wave of Vivian pain.

Her bathroom seemed normal enough, filled with the typical feminine things and touches he'd expected to see. He looked at his watch, wondering how long he could stay there, figuring not more than three or two-and-a-half minutes, since he didn't want her to think he was moving his bowels or anything like that. He took one quick look in the mirror—still didn't like the nervous face he saw there—then spent the rest of his two minutes and twenty seconds looking at the second hand on his wrist-watch, which at least gave him some relief from seeing Vivian's blue-eyed, inescapable face.

He'd intended to say something witty when he returned to the kitchen but was surprised to see her in mid drink with a half-empty bottle of gin beside her on the kitchen counter.

"I'm sorry," she said, after finishing her generous swallow. "I should have waited for you."

"Oh, that's fine," Sidney said, waving his hand dismissively.

"No, it's not. It's rude. I'm being rude. Why don't we go into the living room and have a drink while the chicken's cooking? It'll be ready in another ten minutes."

He thought he should refuse, as he rarely drank, but he also thought it might help his mood to maybe have a few sips.

"Is gin good?" she asked, holding the bottle with a strange smile on her face.

"Whatever you're drinking."

"I could get you some red wine or white."

"Please don't trouble yourself," he said, realizing unequivocally now that she was quite high, and possibly already drunk.

"It's no trouble either way, but it's very sweet of you to worry. So, really, which do you want?"

"Surprise me then," he said, smiling in spite of himself.

"Then you have to go into the living room and sit down on the couch and wait to see what I'll bring."

"This I can do," he said, leaving the kitchen as instructed and sitting under a huge, brightly colored Moët Champagne poster of a man and woman dancing while each is holding an empty glass. Never again would he let David or Viv or anyone else talk him into another date. If Viv stayed with him of course he would never see another woman, and even if she wanted to break up forever he would still never go through this again.

"Ready or not, here I come," Phyllis said, walking into the living room with the gin bottle in one hand and two glasses in the other.

Sidney smiled, thinking these words were more appropriate for a man to say to a woman, that he'd said them to himself a number of times in bed with Viv, especially in their first hot months together, when it seemed he couldn't stop coming, and sometimes did it too soon.

"I see you picked the hard stuff," he said smiling. She looked hurt, as if he was criticizing her, so he quickly said "I'm glad. I could use a real drink."

That's how it began, he would think later, two sad, nervous souls having a drink, trying to get through a date that one way or another had been imposed on them. He remembered thinking that if he listened closely he would find something that he could talk about with her. He was ashamed that he didn't remember what profession she had or if she even had one. That much at least he could discover by listening.

But it didn't turn out that way either. She had two or three more drinks, then started a long monologue that he could barely follow. It was almost as if she were reading from *Finnegans Wake*, only outdoors, while it was raining with a lot of wind. Of course one couldn't expect an improvised speech—the very embodiment, he supposed, of Vivian's "lightness of being"—to have a beginning, middle, and end and to be a well-made story. But still, one did expect to be rewarded with a little coherence every now and then, with some signposts along the way that indicated the general topic of conversation. Instead, the light that came from her speech was intermittent and elusive, like that of fireflies.

He *supposed* she was talking about the men in her past, but that evolved into her somehow praising him, as if they'd had a past together, god forbid!

"You're kind," she was telling him, while he felt he should pinch himself to be sure he wasn't dreaming. "I can tell."

"It so happens that I am," he said, "but how can you tell?"

"The way you talk and the way you look."

"The way I look?"

"You have a kind face and a kind body."

"You mean kind of old and kind of homely?" he said, forcing a laugh.

"No, I meant kind of really attractive."

"Thank you," he said stiffly, remembering with an accompanying stab of pain that it was Vivian who once instructed him to give that simple two-word response to a compliment instead of panicking and putting himself down.

"Kind of very, very, irresistibly attractive," she said, suddenly moving forward so that her head was now resting on his lap.

Sidney stared disbelievingly at the top of her thick, black hair, which seemed young and raw like a wild vegetable.

"You've had a lot to drink," he finally said.

"I've had a lot to think . . . about, and I'm tired of thinking, aren't you?"

Yes, a voice inside him said, I'm tired too. "I just meant . . ."

"Please don't ruin it," she said. "I'm so relieved and happy. The human contact is so nice."

"OK. I understand," he said softly.

"Just do something kind."

"Like for instance?"

"Just touch me, OK? Touch my hair."

He did as he was told, surprised by the rough, foreign texture of it, the first hair besides Vivian's he'd touched in thirteen years.

"I knew you'd have a magic touch, a beautiful touch. I knew the moment I saw you that you were kind and would have a special touch. So I so much want to be nice to you and reward you."

"The chicken dinner is reward enough . . . speaking of which, I think I smell something burning."

"Oh shit! It's probably burned to a crisp by now. I'm sorry."

"I better shut off the oven," he said, getting up abruptly and walking briskly into the kitchen.

"Don't worry," she called out, "I'll order Chinese."

Sure enough, the chicken was witch black, wizened, and smoking. Sidney opened a window to let out the smoke, thanking god that her smoke alarm didn't go off, then reported back to the sofa.

"I'm afraid it's burnt."

"Burnt, ruined, gone. The chicken is gone with the wind."

"Do you want to try to go out for a bite?" Sidney offered, thinking a walk in the cold air along with some food would do her good. She was lying almost completely on her stomach with her eyes closed.

"I'm sorry. I'm so sorry for the chicken that's gone with the wind. Can you forgive me?"

"Of course. This is not a big deal."

"If you bring me the phone, I'll order Chinese."

"I'd be happy to do it for you if you tell me what you want."

"You want me to tell you what I want?"

"Yes, so I can order.

"I want you to sit down where you were before and touch my hair again just like you were before for a few minutes. Then I'll order the food."

Feeling increasingly hungry, Sidney sat down on the sofa. While he patted her hair he stared longingly at the white cordless phone on a table fifteen feet away wishing he could speak to Viv, if only to ask for advice and wishing also he had one of those little cell phones—the size of a candy bar—so he could at least order the Chinese while massaging this strange woman's scalp.

"You really are kind," she was saying half into one of the pink sofa pillows she'd now managed to tuck under her head.

"Do you enjoy being kind?"

"It's just the way I am," Sidney said, "though people usually don't describe it the way you do."

"A lot of men don't, you know."

"Don't what?"

"Enjoy being kind. To them you're just like some product on a conveyor belt. They'll maybe pick you up and use you to see if you work to their specif . . ."

"Specifications?"

"Yuh, and then they'll put you back on the belt and watch you get sealed up and packaged."

He was losing Phyllis again, he felt he was losing everything. Tonight he wouldn't call Viv and ask permission to speak. Instead he'd go straight to her apartment, *their* apartment, and demand to see her. She thought he never rocked the boat—well, he would rock it this time. He would tell her he loved her and she had to make a decision, that all this indecisiveness and dating nonsense was making him meshuga.

Phyllis had started another monologue, this one like a softer *Finnegans Wake*, a *Finnegans Wake* lullaby, Sidney thought. He let her talk without interruption, feeling that it was calming her down. When it would end he'd tell her about Vivian, perhaps even how she insisted on his dating again, but at any rate about how he never should have done it because of the pain he was still in, pain that he knew would never end. He would tell Phyllis she was a lovely person, that she was attractive, which she was, and he would offer friendship and then he would shake her hand, perhaps hug her if she wanted, and assure her he'd enjoyed their meeting, trying hard to sound sincere so later, when she remembered some of this, she wouldn't feel too bad.

Phyllis was still talking and Sidney, hearing his name, began to listen to a few lines. "Sidney, you've been such a mensch. How can I repay you? Can you think of a way? Can I give you a kiss? Sidney, can I? Can I show you what I made for you? I think you'll like it when you see it. Should I show you?"

Had she made a pie or some other dessert for him? He wouldn't mind a piece.

"Is it something in the kitchen?" he asked. There was no answer and he wondered if he'd made some kind of faux pas. Then he looked down and realized that she'd fallen asleep and was, in fact, already snoring rather loudly. What should he do? She might sleep for hours and then it would be too late to go to Viv's.

He got up from the sofa carefully, almost tiptoeing, as he looked for and finally found some stationery and a ballpoint pen on a desk in her office. He wrote hurriedly so that he had to throw away the first draft of the speech he'd rehearsed in his head a few minutes before about not being ready to date. He felt vaguely like a criminal writing it in her office, as if this space, which she'd never showed him, was taboo, and tried not to look at her papers or at any of the photographs on the desk. But one caught his eye. It was of a lovely little brown-haired girl on a beach— perhaps a beach in Cape Cod. Did Phyllis have a daughter or was this a photograph of herself when she was younger? How strange time must be when you have children, Sidney thought wistfully. The way the future merges and blurs with the past. Then he finished the note and placed it on the sofa next to the sleeping woman, still tiptoeing toward the door and wondering, as he softly closed it, exactly what it was she'd wanted to show him.

He took it as a good omen that he found a cab right away. There was no time to call Viv, no time to be polite or hesitant. Of course by surprising her at night like this he ran several risks. She could well be out herself, for instance, at the movies or the gym or on one of her health walks. Still worse, of course, she could be with a man in the apartment, but then he would at least know what was going on—his tortured guessing games would finally stop—and if it came to that he could just pass out, as Phyllis had. Ah, poor Phyllis. He would definitely call her tomorrow, explain, apologize, offer to be friends.

The cab reached the outskirts of Harvard Square, the lights of Cambridge even more crowded than the lights of Boston. It drove by Harvard Yard, so dark and vast it seemed to eat almost all the lights, and then onto Cambridge Street, where their apartment was.

Of course Viv would never let it come to that, never let him actually walk in on her with another man. She controlled the buzzer and right now had both keys. So his nightmare couldn't really happen, could it?

Sidney left the driver a generous tip, as if for good luck, and walked directly toward the apartment. His heart was beating too fast, he thought, so he took two big breaths.

"Oh, hi Sidney," a woman said, smiling. It was Joan, their neighbor from upstairs. "Coming in?" she said, holding the door open for him.

"Thank you," he said.

So he would bypass the buzzers after all and knock directly on her door. He could barely understand what Joan was saying to him in the elevator and could only mumble "thanks again" and "goodnight."

This is the end of reality, Sidney thought, or the beginning. He knocked twice and got no answer, knocked again and waited.

"Who is it?" came the voice at last. Her voice.

"It's the big bad wolf and if you don't let me in I'll huff and I'll puff and I'll blow your door down."

She opened the door wearing his favorite blue dress, which set off her eyes so well. She was smiling though there may have been a tear or two in her eyes.

"Come in," she said. "I'm so glad it's you." They stared at each other for a few seconds, then she slowly extended her arms and embraced him.

"I'm really so glad to see you," she said. "So glad to stop fighting with you."

He could feel her breathing, almost vibrating, like her kitten did sometimes when he held it against himself.

"Glad doesn't begin to describe how I feel," he said. "I was afraid that when I got here . . ."

"Shh," she said cutting him off. "I thought the big bad wolf was never afraid."

"The Jewish big bad wolf sometimes is . . . I mean, I must have surprised you."

"It was kind of surprising that you didn't call. So, how come no call first?"

"The big bad wolf doesn't do calls."

Vivian laughed and continued to hold him.

"So, how was your date? The first and last date I'll ever allow you to have."

"*This* is my date, my date forever with you, my beauty queen. What do you say?"

"I say I like this big bad wolf's approach and I'm really sorry I've been a little pig for such a long time."

"Your extreme beauty and wonderful taste compels me to forgive you, little pig."

"But, I want to do something to make it up to you wolf, what could it be?"

"I'm very hungry," he said, lowering his hand down her back.

"For what kind of food?"

"First you, my darling pig, then kreplach."

ROBERT AND HIS WIFE

I'd been coming to the meetings for some time. I would sit and listen and occasionally talk from the couch or straight-back chair in a poorly lit living room. We had rotating hosts but all the living rooms looked more or less alike, with paintings and posters and plants and cats and Satie or Miles Davis in the background when we first walked in. There would also be chocolate-chip cookies, cheese and crackers, and cheap wine on a table. When there was something in my life I wouldn't go but when there was nothing I went. It was true that there were no particularly attractive women at the meetings and it was also pretty sad to hear the mostly middle-aged members reading their stories and poems that no one would ever publish, but there were times when I simply needed to listen and talk to people so I went, though I never wrote anything for the group myself.

With no potential love interest at the meetings, I began to focus my attention on Robert, who by acclamation was the group's most interesting person. One night Robert read one of his stories. I remember the first two lines were "There are lonely people and people who don't know they're lonely. Derek was a little of both."

Not bad lines, I thought. They stuck in my mind though I couldn't tell you much about the rest of the story. Those lines, however, made me decide to talk to him that night, and as soon as the meeting was over I invited him over for a drink at the Majestic, our neighborhood restaurant/bar.

Robert is a large man with a big flowing beard. Since I'm thin and clean-shaven with much shorter hair, we're pretty much physical opposites. The only physical thing we have in common is the tinge of gray at our temples.

After our drinks came I felt I should say something more about his story but was afraid he'd realize I hadn't paid much attention past the opening lines. Instead I took a swallow of my whisky sour and said, "Sometimes, even when the meetings go on too long, I don't like them to end 'cause I just don't want to be in my apartment. Of course I don't say much in the group . . . you may have noticed I have trouble writing stories."

"Your writing will come when it comes," Robert said softly. Then he looked at me a moment. "I know what you mean about not wanting to face your apartment. I've certainly been there."

"Really? When was that? I picture you always with friends. Everyone in the group seems to gravitate toward you."

"After my divorce, I felt that way. And not just about my apartment. If somebody held up a line in the grocery store 'cause their credit card wouldn't work, I'd be seething, like I was ready to strangle them. I had a *very* short fuse with people then but I didn't want to be alone either."

I was surprised to hear this. I was almost disoriented in a way, since Robert seemed so calm and self-possessed—a man always on top of things. I asked him what got him over it.

"Becoming friends with Beth again, my ex-wife, helped a lot. That didn't make the divorce such a loss. It was also much better for our children too, even though at the time they were almost grown."

Robert, I found out, had two daughters. One had just started law school, the other was two years into medical school. He described his relationship with them as "very close." When I asked if he was still friends with his ex-wife he quickly said, "Oh yes. Great, very close friends. She still lives near St. Louis, in Clayton. She's in a writer's group there as a matter of fact. You'd like Beth. Everyone does."

I nodded. I'd wanted to say something but didn't. He went on to tell me more about Beth. She was an intense this, she was a sensitive that. She was a thinker, too, who'd majored in philosophy in college. She'd influenced his own philosophy, probably too grand a word Robert conceded, correcting himself, let's say his view of the world. "What view is that?" I asked.

He went on to explain about feeling eternity in a moment as a way of compensating for death. I didn't really understand. It didn't mean much to me, but I kept asking him questions. I realized I was afraid to talk because I wanted Robert to think well of me intellectually, since I thought of him as my intellectual superior, at least in an IQ sort of way. I thanked him for discussing his view of things. He'd certainly given me lots to think about, I said. Then I paused, wondering what we would talk about next when Robert suddenly said, "So, Gerry, is there anyone special in your life these days?"

"No, no one special," I said. Wasn't that obvious from what I'd just said? I thought.

"Well, I've definitely been there," Robert said.

Of course you've been there, I thought. You've been everywhere, you're ubiquitous.

"So, how did you handle it?" I said, thinking that he wanted me to ask him.

"Different ways. Sometimes I did the singles ads. Have you ever thought of doing something along those lines?"

"Not really. I've done it but I don't quite have the heart for it right now."

"I hear you. You know you could meet Beth, if you like. You could probably go out with her."

I didn't say anything to that. I think I began blinking to hide how upset I was. Then I thanked him at least two more times. "Let me think about it. It's really nice for you to offer," I said. I changed the subject finally, and ten minutes of chitchat later I left the bar with him and said goodnight.

I was rattled and didn't answer my doorman when he said hello to me. I stood in my living room looking at the snow around the trees in the park across the street—first from a distance, then up close—like a person in a museum who keeps moving between a place where he sees a painting in perspective to one in which he sees the brush strokes in detail. I simply couldn't keep still, I was so shaken by Robert's offer. I thought he must be very secure with himself sexually to make such a proposal. He must not be afraid at all of being compared to me or of having to see me in the group knowing that his wife might have slept with me and be comparing us. Obviously I didn't inspire any fear in him, or else he was simply beyond those bourgeois feelings. The bottom line was by making the offer he'd vanquished me, in a way, and showed himself to be completely superior to me. I was but a flake of common snow and he the huge tree I clung to even as it towered over me.

How easy life is for people who see things in a clear-cut way and become, as a result, clear-cut themselves. Robert struck me as a clear-cut man, whereas everything about me was ambiguous and ambivalent. There were, for example, three women in my life (including my ex-wife, who'd divorced me before we had any children) with whom I had ambiguous friendships. I would feel romantic impulses in each case but also anger and so couldn't bring myself to take it to the next plane with any of them. Robert, on the other hand, had so clearly and decisively resolved things with his ex that he could offer her to me, a casual friend at best. Similarly, I loathed my job at the library, yet found it difficult to pursue any other work or serious use of my energy. In the group I hadn't written two sentences whereas Robert, who was in the real estate business and loved it, had made the transition to the group seamlessly, not only writing more prolifically and better than anyone else but also commenting the most expansively and sensitively about other people's work and thus becoming the most gregarious, popular, and respected person at the meetings.

It shouldn't have come as any surprise to me, now that I thought about it, that his worldview was also clear-cut and stated in a soft but confident manner. He believed it without being fanatical about it. I didn't believe in it or in any other quasi-comforting metaphysical ideas yet felt that revealed a defect in me more than anything else. I was not, as I was currently constituted, psychologically equipped to believe in anything that was too comforting.

That night I spent an unsettling time trying to find some value in my apartment, which I generally ignored, or at least in some of my possessions, such as a rather pedestrian lithograph I'd bought on a trip to Boston, or my blue reclining chair in the living room, which I'd inherited from my parents, or even my old-fashioned-looking bedding, which one of my former girlfriends had got me for Christmas years ago. Though I'd never seen it, I soon found myself imagining Robert's apartment and his most treasured possessions and began comparing them to mine. I thought he probably had a fireplace in his living room and paintings on the wall which artist friends had given him—paintings which, while short of Cézanne or Van Gogh, showed flashes of real talent and passion and which, despite a certain amateurish quality here and there that ultimately made them all the more touching, were works of real distinction.

His furniture would definitely not be ostentatious. There would be no Formica or plastic, either, even in the kitchen (as was the case with mine). Instead, there would be fine wooden chairs. And the bedroom, where his naked lovers swooned and kissed his beard there would be, what? I couldn't tell, I wasn't able to imagine such a room, though I kept imagining the women who invested so much time there—time they were always grateful for. Hard-bodied, independent, no-nonsense women who were devoted to Robert out of strength, not weakness.

It wasn't easy to sleep that night. My usual cocktail of Ativan and TV had to be supplemented by beer and extra-strength Tylenol. I was not a whiz at the library the next day, either. When my daydreams about Robert's apartment continued the next night, I found myself reaching for the phone and calling him. What was it exactly I wanted to say? I didn't know, other than to first of all apologize for calling him so late. Then finally, as an excuse for calling, I told him I'd been thinking about his philosophy a lot, puzzling over it, especially his concept of eternity in a moment. If he could he possibly explain it again, I'd be most grateful.

Robert paused a second and began to explain. He was, of course, much less formal on the phone than me, since he was taking me at face value and answering me sincerely, whereas I was once again essentially deceiving him.

"First of all, I'm not real comfortable with calling it a philosophy. Who knows what philosophy is anymore, anyway?" Robert said.

"Exactly. So why not call it one?"

He laughed a little, probably stroked his beard thoughtfully, then said "point taken, but I still don't know that I want to dignify it with a term like philosophy. They're just feelings I have, that Beth had first actually, then kind of imparted to me, about how to deal with the death problem . . ."

"The death problem?"

"Our awareness of death, which we see as the key issue of man's situation. There, is that pompous enough for you? I mean the main societal response to death appears to be the creation of religions, almost all of which offer immortality as a way of dealing with it, but Beth and I don't believe in a life to come."

"As Beckett said, 'mine was always that,'" I added, unable to resist displaying a little of my librarian's erudition.

"Good one. That's a good quote. Anyway, we don't believe in an afterlife but we *do* believe in eternity in a moment—certain special moments or epiphanies during which we experience a sense of timelessness and so defeat death—at least for a while." He paused then, perhaps sensing that I wasn't buying it, yet he stayed patient and continued to speak about it in more detail. Obviously, he loved the challenge of enlightening me. I waited him out, thanked him in an appropriately convincing manner an appropriately convincing number of times, and then asked if I could take him to lunch sometime during the week. We settled on the Majestic two days later.

At lunch, I again had to face my embarrassing emptiness of purpose, but Robert showed no signs of puzzling over it. It was as if his eyes (and matching shirt) summed him up: sky blue and innocent. He assumed it was simply that I liked him, I suppose. He took a big swallow of ham and eggs, unselfconsciously licking up a little of the runny yolk from his bottom lip and said, "I've got a date after lunch with a great lady I'm really excited about. Her name is Sherry, and we're going to meet at her house."

"How did this happen?" I asked.

"Just by chance. We were at Left Bank Books and were reaching for the same novel by Günter Grass at the same time. Then we started laughing at the coincidence."

"Then talking and so on . . ."

"Yes, just spontaneously like that. Couldn't have planned it better."

"If I'd been in that bookstore looking for something German I would have gone to Thomas Bernhard and I wouldn't have met anyone because people don't know about him, much less read him."

"Thomas Bernhard?" Robert said, looking puzzled.

"My point exactly," I said. "But you should read him."

"I will, I will. Anyway, I'm just floating now because of Sherry."

"The Günter Grass girl."

"Yes, just floating. We've had two terrific dates and now I'm going to meet her at her place."

I noticed that he'd gone from eating his eggs fairly rapidly to virtually attacking them, as he would no doubt be passionately using his mouth with Sherry Grass in the immediate future. I wished him well, of course, and forced myself to laugh and congratulate him on his good fortune. He laughed in his Robert style, then said, "Hey, Gerry, I brought something for you."

"What's that?"

He opened his wallet and handed me a photograph of a voluptuous blonde woman in a bathing suit standing by a lake.

"I brought a picture of Beth for you to see. What do you think?"

"Nice looking," I said.

"Remember, she's just a phone call away."

"What makes you think she'd like me?"

"I like you a lot and we usually like the same people."

"And you're sure your relationship with her is over, you don't ever think about going back?"

"No, no, that was all resolved a long time ago. I love Beth, that will never end, but it's a different kind of love now so it's on to new adventures for me and now that I've already had them I want the same for her too."

"That's very generous of you, very mature."

"I think you need to go on to new adventures too," Robert said to me. "I think something inside you is holding you back like an emotional seat belt, and now you need to unbuckle it once and for all."

I looked up from my Caesar salad.

"I know you well enough that I can talk to you this way, don't you think?"

"Sure," I said, although I didn't think he really did.

"I don't know which way you're gonna end up loving Beth but you *will* love her—she's one great lady, so I've gone ahead and made plans for the four of us, Sherry and me and you and Beth, to have dinner at Cardwell's together this Friday night, unless you already have other plans or just really don't want to do it. Like the ad says, 'Life Beckons,' so what do you say?"

It was a question I would repeat to myself many times that night in my apartment, though always with an answer different from the timid go-ahead (accompanied by my humble thanks) I gave to Robert that afternoon.

"Great news! Good decision," he'd bellowed. "You know you reminded me of someone who really wants to go swimming but can't get himself to jump in the water so I just gave you a little push," he said, with his big manly laugh. I forced myself to laugh too, of course.

. . . .

With Cardwell's, Robert had picked an overtly romantic restaurant for the occasion, dark, and lit by candles reflected in the wide mirrors that covered the walls. I arrived, overdressed compared to Robert and company, and feeling tense, apprehensive, and secretly angry at a lot of things. I was angry at Robert for being so controlling and even angrier at myself for the way I'd caved in to his grand plan, which struck me from the start more as a grand illusion. Now I would be trapped in a restaurant with one woman who loved Robert in the past (and probably always would) and another who loved him in the present. I would doubtlessly end up drooling over both while each would always be out of reach for me because each (as Robert well knew on some level) was perpetually in Robert's grasp.

I arrived no more than three minutes late but they were all already seated and laughing and had already ordered a drink that was also waiting for me.

"Here's the man," Robert said in his hearty, utterly earnest voice, and for a moment I actually felt like someone important, I have to admit. But the feeling quickly disappeared. Everyone was smiling in a way that almost blinded me (perhaps the candlelight somehow enhanced the whiteness of all the straight teeth that were directed at me). Then my feeling of well-being dissolved completely as I was struck by the sisterly resemblance of the two blonde women and their synchronized smiles. Beth, seated next to me, was the older "sister," of course, but still very attractive (as I knew she would be) in her beige suit, which couldn't hide her full breasts and natural curves. Yes, she was a true middle-aged treasure, I thought.

Sherry, who I later found out was fourteen years younger than Beth, had almost the same shade of hair, perhaps a degree or two lighter, and similar sky-blue eyes—which, as a matter of fact, was the color of Robert's eyes as well. She was a little slimmer looking in her hip-hugging jeans and orange sweater, but there was enough resemblance that someone seeing them for the first time would probably conclude that they were from the same family, which in a way they were. They were Robertites—with tight, beautiful bodies and faces and sharp, clear, liberated minds. All this was immediately obvious by the way Robert unselfconsciously had his arm around Sherry's shoulder, which didn't appear to faze Beth a bit. Ah, to have everything so well resolved, to be able to laugh at one's loss and embrace the new, to have a lifetime of eternal moments each one following the other as in a waterfall or a fugue, that was the Robert way. No wonder they were all laughing, Beth and Beth past (aka Sherry) and the happy philosopher Robert himself, who laughed the loudest of all.

The food came and it was excellent. My angel-hair shrimp was particularly tasty, and everyone else's food was first-rate. (Robert proposed that we all share, so of course we all did.) The first ten minutes or so I began to enjoy myself again because of the food but also because of the group banter, which was light but witty. We didn't talk about Iraq or Social Security or any of the other big issues of the day, but we managed to reassure ourselves that we were all intelligent—or at least intelligent enough to entertain each other through dinner.

But Phase Two, as I thought of it in my subsequent postdinner analysis, was very different. In Phase Two we, in effect, sectioned off into couples, Robert talking to Sherry and Beth talking to me. It was so smooth a transition it was almost as if Robert were conducting us, though I never saw an actual baton. Perhaps he signaled his impeccably rehearsed women with the raising of one of his prominent eyebrows or perhaps with one of his innocent midwestern winks—I couldn't tell but that hardly mattered. They could.

"Robert tells me you grew up in the East," Beth said to me, "What part?"

"Very near Boston, in a town called Brookline."

"Oh. We loved Brookline. Robert has an old college buddy we visited there, and Boston is just magnificent. When did you move to St. Louis?"

"Seven years ago," I said, then quickly added, "Are you from St. Louis?"

"No, we're westerners, originally. First Seattle then Santa Cruz, spent some time in Denver and Salt Lake City too. Robert and me are from all over, I guess, but I think we've both found our home here at last."

(Only later, during my close-to-sleepless night, did I realize that she kept referring to Robert as if he were still her husband even as he was massaging Sherry at the same table in one erogenous zone after another.)

Then it happened. Beth asked me the inevitable question of what I did for a living (I was surprised Robert hadn't already briefed her on that) and at the moment she asked it, Robert and Sherry suddenly stopped talking and turned toward me to listen as if an important announcement were about to begin. (I would have lied, perhaps, had they not stopped to listen, but Robert already knew the truth.) So it was I had to say the word *librarian* in front of both women, and the reluctant way I said it only underscored the humiliation I felt in front of the successful real estate man and his female posse. All this must have been somewhat shocking for Sherry, who let out a little gasp, while Beth merely looked stricken. Of course it's possible that I misperceived these reactions or exaggerated them—I only report, like everyone else, what I believe I experienced.

Beth, being the more sensitive of Robert's women, tried to help me recover by changing the subject, because what could you say to a middle-aged male librarian who wanted to be something else, to make him feel better? My work was neither important nor exciting nor in any way controversial, as everyone everywhere knows.

"Robert told me you're in the same writing group as he is." (*That* she remembered, of course.) "You must really love literature."

I nodded without saying a word. It was as if I were enveloped in an invisible but noxious cloud that prevented me from speaking.

"What are you writing now?" was her next question, asked no doubt to allow me to talk about something I liked. But as I had yet to write even a complete paragraph since joining the group, as Robert knew, my humiliation was now complete.

"A number of things," I said, looking down at the table. "But I haven't handed anything in to the group yet."

When I looked up, that little expression of compassion that I hated to see was in her eyes again. It seemed that she was sizing me up pretty quickly.

"Robert tells me that your group is really cool."

"Yes, they're a nice group of people . . . and, of course, that's how I met Robert."

"I met Robert in a literary way, too," Sherry suddenly said, who unbeknownst to me was apparently still listening to my fumbling conversation with Beth. I should have said, "I know, Robert already told me how you met, ad nauseam." Instead I looked at her quizzically, trying to hide my shock at just how young and beautiful she truly was, so beautiful that I immediately looked away again, first at Robert, who was smiling self-satisfiedly, then at a point just past his happy head. (I was afraid, of course, to look at Beth.)

"We were in a bookstore and were reaching for the same book at the same time."

I wondered again if their hands actually touched on the Grass cover, if they touched before they even spoke.

"Not only that but when we realized what happened we both started laughing at exactly the same time."

Of course, everything with them happened simultaneously.

"Incredible," I said, as Robert winked at me.

I was fully inside my noxious cloud waiting for a wind to carry me away, but the wind never came. It was like being in a horror movie that wouldn't end, whose script I was discovering as the horror kept happening. We stayed there eating and drinking till midnight as I felt what I used to think of as my soul drain away. When it finally ended Robert gave me a big bear hug and reminded me that if we didn't meet for lunch before, he'd see me in his apartment in a week, as it was his turn to host the next group meeting.

"Great, I'll be very curious to see your apartment," I said, as I got into my car. So, I would finally get to see his home instead of just imagining it on a nightly basis, just as I had finally seen Robert's wife, instead of just the photograph, and then Robert's young girlfriend, instead of just his frenzied words describing her. These were the ironic rewards of my life.

I needed still more alcohol to be able to sleep that night. It was the first of six straight nights that I drank in my apartment before the group met at Robert's home. On the second of those nights I did a foolish thing. Around ten o'clock, after a glass and a half of wine, I looked up Beth in the phone book. I assumed correctly that she was still listed under her married name, then I called her, listened to her say hello a few times, and hung up. (Of course I pressed *67 before dialing so that my call would be untraceable.) It was hard to know why I called and hung up like that—the kind of thing I hadn't done in thirty years. At first, I tried to laugh it off, but it began to bother me more and more and I soon found it necessary to call Robert.

I apologized for calling so late and, of course, he told me not to worry, that he and Sherry were about to play a game of Scrabble, of all things. I quickly got to the point, and asked him if he was free for lunch tomorrow. "Of course," he said, without a moment's hesitation. "Where would you like to meet?"

Once again we met at the Majestic, this time at high noon. We both ordered gyro platters while I waited for him to tell me if he'd talked with Beth about me. Instead, ever-direct Robert asked me what *I* thought of Beth.

"She's very nice, and Sherry is too."

"Well, Gerry, the ball's in your court now," Robert said, smiling broadly.

"Did she happen to say anything to you about me?" I finally said, unable to wait any longer. For the first time Robert avoided my eyes when he answered.

"Oh, she thinks you're real nice too. I knew she would."

"How did you know that?" I said in a way that forced him to look at me.

"Because let's face it, big guy, you're a pretty nice fellah."

Maybe he meant to encourage me, maybe not, but the word *nice* said with averted eyes and without any other supporting descriptors, such as she also thinks you're hot, cute, good-looking, sexy, or at least attractive, I quickly translated into—her interest is platonic, she basically wants a new person to talk to about Robert. That invisible cloud, the noxious one, slipped over me again and I was emotionally absent for the rest of the lunch.

. . . .

I had always been a bit disengaged at the library, but in the week before the group meeting at Robert's I was quasi-dysfunctional. It was almost as if I kept blacking out and would wake up wondering what I was doing there. Other times I would sit at my desk without a thought in my head as if I were a fish who somehow had slipped on a human disguise.

At night, especially after I began to drink, I came alive again, though I'd inevitably find myself on Planet Robert, thinking endlessly about him and his women, for one couldn't think about any one of the trinity without thinking of the others. For example, I'd begin by focusing on Robert's lovemaking sessions with Sherry. It occurred to me, while I thought of that, that Robert, having been married so long, and having two children and still being very good friends with his ex-wife, and also being the kind of Robert he was—confident, liberal, and adventuresome—had probably had the type of sex life where he did *everything* with Beth, and learned to do it all superbly, and was now overwhelming Sherry with his sex and life skills. This overwhelming ability of his would, of course, bind Sherry to him from the start, slavishly and completely. Yet, it was all traceable ultimately to his ex-wife Beth, whom Robert had blithely offered me. When I'd try to isolate Beth and think solely of her I'd find her alternately beautiful and repellent. I'd feel attracted but also angry at her as if, absurdly enough, she'd stabbed me in the back by marrying Robert and sleeping with him all those years. Then that realization in turn led me to imagining his years of lovemaking with Beth, with whom he had honed his Robert art of love.

Even in my dreams I couldn't escape them. I would dream of making love with Beth only to have Robert walk through the door with an anxious look on his face. Once I dreamed I went on vacation with the three of them where I granted myself both his women only to have Robert interrupt me once again.

. . . .

Then, on the eve of the writer's meeting, I had an uneasy night of dreams about following Robert in the snow—the horizon lined with icicles hanging from the clouds like the teeth of whales and then somehow, as if there were no day at the library in between, I was in Robert's apartment. Of course there *was* a day. I believed too much in common sense to think one hadn't bothered to show up, but I couldn't, nor can I now, remember, one moment of it. I must have dressed and then found myself at the meeting in Robert's apartment, extremely grateful that neither Beth nor Sherry was there. Instead, there was Libby in a purple dress, who wrote devotional sonnets about the animals in her life, holding a plastic glass of white wine, and there (by the fireplace!) was Donald, the accountant, in his horn-rimmed glasses, trying to find a woman to talk with him. Donald, who in his other life wrote ghost stories that, alas, were neither scary nor funny. And there was Marie, the postmodernist, with her unwaxed mustache talking first with me for a moment and then with stream-of-consciousness Roger, the James Joyce devotee who wrote more like Joyce Brothers, I'm afraid. Finally, dressed in a flannel shirt and jeans like the mountain man come down to lead us to the promised land was Robert, rounding us up and even clapping his hands like a scout master to get our attention. "Come on," he said, "the bus is leaving. I'm going to take you all on the grand two-minute tour of the apartment so you can see some changes I've made."

His apartment was not exactly as I had imagined it, but it was enough like it to make me wonder about my daydreams. There were fine wooden chairs, but more in the living room than in the kitchen. There was the fireplace, of course, and while there were no paintings of the type I had imagined, there was a large family portrait in the living room—Robert, wife and daughters, all looking quite earnest and beautiful—that Robert told me had been painted by an old friend.

His bedroom, slightly smaller than I'd pictured yet wonderful in its austerity, had a photograph of Robert and wife on his bed table. She had an inviting smile and Robert's arm was tightly around her. Then, on the wall above his bed, I saw a small nude of a blond with a particularly alluring upper body. While her face was turned and hidden by her yellow hair, I assumed it was another painting of his wife. Apparently Sherry was too mature to object, or perhaps a painting of her had already been commissioned and would soon be on the wall next to it.

"Beth?" I found myself asking him softly, though I immediately wished I hadn't.

"Yes," Robert said, smiling and showing no trace of embarrassment.

"Painted by the same friend who did the family portrait?"

"Yes, it's by Kenneth, an old friend from college. We had summer cottages next to each other in Nantucket once. I miss old Ken."

Perhaps I had predecessors, I thought, as we all filed back into the living room and resumed our seats on Robert's furniture. In fact, I thought about it intermittently during Marie's pointlessly gnarled "story," then during Roger's plotless stream-of-consciousness babble. But even more, far more, I thought about Robert himself, and his women. They were strange thoughts and lasted longer than strange thoughts usually do. I thought about how wives never really leave you, as mine hadn't completely left me. How nothing like that ever ends. Yet in my case there was an ambiguous, ultimately unsatisfactory "friendship," whereas in Robert's case he and his wife were permanently joined together through their children (which I hadn't had, though I'd wanted to) and even through the new woman Robert was sleeping with, who looked like a younger version of his wife. I remember thinking that about Sherry the second I met her. It's his wife again, only the grass is greener. So green that Robert could offer me his wife, but in a way that humiliated me, which I was bound to refuse because he'd made it obvious that they were eternally fused, that she was irreplaceable to him, and that no one could get as close, could perhaps even become close enough to him to get a *part* of him, unless it was through his wife in one way or another.

I felt agitated, uneasy. Libby was reading, I think, when I excused myself to go to the bathroom. But I didn't stay there long. I felt a tremendous sense of injustice sweep over me thinking, in fact becoming convinced, that this perfect man was lying to me and was still sleeping with his wife.

It was as if I could sense, even smell, the sex they had had in the bathroom which, in turn, explained his offer to me. There was no chance I could succeed with her because he was still with Sherry Grass *and* Beth.

I thought about flushing the toilet to create a camouflage but realized no one would hear it above the group noise and no one was keeping track of my doings, anyway. I had at least three more minutes, I figured, maybe five.

I kept walking, albeit lightly, into his bedroom. The bed table lamp was still on. I looked at the photograph and a cold shiver went through me. I mentally measured it. Then I picked it up and discovered I could fit it, frame and all, underneath my sweater. That would have been it but then I realized he would probably know it was me, yet being Robert might not even care enough to confront me about it.

There were a couple of minutes left. I began opening and shutting bureau drawers. Finally I found it shining in its case at the back of drawer number two. It was a gold wedding band of fairly high quality. I picked it up and read the inscription "Love forever, your Beth." Then I put it in my pocket. How does this fit into your philosophy, I said to Robert in my mind. Then I checked to see that all the doors were shut and tried to wipe off where I imagined my fingerprints were with the sleeve of my sweater. When I rejoined the group it was obliviously jabbering away about Libby's latest animal sonnet.

I remember virtually nothing of the rest of the meeting. Maybe only a vague image of Robert in his magnificent beard and flannel shirt. I do remember being hyper-conscious of the ring in my pocket. Also, there was no more thinking about Robert's wife and all that she meant. It was as if I had her in my pocket too.

I'm sure I waited till the end before saying goodbye to each group member in as normal a manner as possible. I said goodbye to Robert too and made a point of shaking his hand, though I thought my own hand was acting a little nervous. He looked at me as if he half expected me to ask him to go out for another drink. But that could wait. I wanted to get home as soon as possible.

He got off easy, I thought as I walked home through the snow under the near-full moon. I didn't think about how long it would take him to discover it was gone (perhaps he looked at it or touched his ring every night for all I knew), nor how long before he'd call the police or me. In my lobby, I once more walked by my doorman without saying hello.

I wanted lots of light to look at it properly and thought I would turn on all of them. But once in my apartment I changed my mind. Instead, I found myself drawn to the picture window in the living room. The blinds were up, and outside I could see the snow around the trees in the park, looping over their branches now as well. Finally, I had something shining inside my apartment, I thought, as I took out the ring and held it against the window. The phone was ringing, but I never thought of answering it. I was staring at my shining ring against a field of snow and stars completely immersed in my eternal moment.

MAYOR BAT

"Where am I?"

"You were asleep," the man said. "I just woke you up."

"Really?"

"Yes, really."

"I must have passed out. I'm sorry."

"That's fine, I didn't mind. It was kind of peaceful, though I'm definitely glad you're awake now."

"Why were you driving so long?" the woman asked.

"Was it so long? Come on, open your door, let's get out."

Outside it was extremely dark and they could hear the wind blowing through the trees around the parking lot.

He walked around the car and took her hand.

"Where are we?"

"Wonderland," he said lightly.

"I believe it," she said. "We must be way out in the middle of nowhere."

"When we were in Philly you only thought it was night. Now you know what night really looks like."

He opened a door at street level and they walked into the apartment.

"Jesus Christ, it's even darker in here. How can you see?"

"Because I'm Mayor Bat, the mayor of Wonderland."

"OK, Mr. Mayor, could you turn on a light?"

He walked straight ahead and turned on a dim lamp at the end of the living room. Then he went into the adjoining kitchen. "You want something to drink?" he said, opening the refrigerator, "or would you like something else?"

"Yes, sure."

"Yes, sure, what?"

"Yes to both of them," she said, laughing and following him into the kitchen. "I need to get back into a wonderland kind of mood."

He looked at her. He was struck by how skinny she was (somehow in the bar she didn't look that thin), although she did have a figure. "OK, Alice, I'll see what I can do."

"Hey, who's Alice? You don't even remember my name, do you?"

"You're Alice in Wonderland, aren't you?"

"Oh, OK. I get it," she said, taking the glass of vodka and tonic he'd poured her and immediately beginning to drink it.

"So which character are you, the Mad Hatter?"

"I'm Lewis Carroll."

"Who's he? I don't remember any Lewis Carroll."

"He wrote the book. He was an Englishman who liked little girls, especially a little girl named Alice, so he wrote a book about her."

She took a big swallow of her drink until it was practically gone. "So you think I'm just a little girl?"

"Not at all," he said. "You don't look like one and you don't kiss like one either. Come on, finish your drink."

"Why aren't you drinking?"

"I'm gonna smoke. With you. It's not easy being Lewis Carroll."

"I'll bet," she said.

. . . .

They were in the bedroom, where there wasn't much light either, smoking a joint. The room didn't seem to have any secrets or even any personality, she thought. There weren't any pictures anywhere, or even a TV. Just a generic kind of bureau and bed table, where the ashtray was, and a mirror on the wall. It looked more like a nondescript motel room than someone's bedroom, except that the walls looked thick and distorted, different somehow. She thought of asking him about the walls but was afraid he might take offense. When she went out, especially to bars, she invariably wound up with nothing or with nothing men, but Gordon seemed different, funny and smart. He'd made her laugh a lot in the bar and he really seemed to like her, so she wanted to be careful with him. The only thing about him that got on her nerves was the way he kept calling her Alice, but it also seemed too late to say anything about that.

"Here, Alice," he said, handing her the joint. "Finish it."

She took the joint and inhaled. The thing about drinking was you usually laughed a lot because things suddenly seemed so light and funny, but when you smoked pot, especially right after drinking, it was often like going down a slide and landing in a serious and silent world where the quiet could only be broken by sex. She braced herself for that quiet and was relieved when he finally said something.

"Can I tell you what I'm thinking?"

"Yah, sure, I'd like to hear."

They were lying on his bed with their clothes on, so far not touching.

"I was thinking about what things in the world are really poetic and I came to the conclusion that the most poetic thing in the world must be the love between a father and his son, especially when the son is young, like six or seven or eight years old."

"What about between a mother and her son?"

"No, then it's too sexual, all that oedipal stuff ruins it. It may be more intense but it's not as poetic. *Capice?*"

"What's '*capice*' mean?"

"It means 'do you understand?' It's an Italian expression."

"Are you Italian?"

"No. I don't look Italian, do I?"

"No, I guess you don't."

"So what do I look like, what nationality, I mean?"

"I don't know . . . You look like the mayor of Wonderland."

"Is that good? Does that turn you on?

"I wouldn't have kissed you if you didn't."

"But you haven't done that for a while."

"You could do something about that," she said, thinking what do you expect me to do when you're doing all this talking about "poetic" things?

When they started to kiss she realized again how dark and quiet it was and couldn't tell if it was disturbing or exciting. She was pretty high and guessed that was why her feelings kept changing. She wondered what he was feeling, too, but it was difficult to tell. He was going about his business in a quiet way, maybe because he was stoned too. She thought that she still didn't know where she was, but how could she ask him now that he was unhooking her bra? As soon as it was over she would ask him again and make him tell her. It was too weird otherwise. She'd always at least known where she made love in the past. If she didn't, it would be like doing it in empty space.

· · · · · · · · ·

"Hey, what are you doing?" she said. He was sitting on her, wearing only his underpants (he was at least sixty pounds heavier than her, she figured, heavier than he'd looked in the bar), one knee pressing hard on each of her biceps. It was about five minutes after they'd had sex, maybe less.

"Come on, get off me, it hurts."

He didn't answer, just looked at her, although it was dark enough that she couldn't be sure exactly where he was looking.

"I mean it, it really hurts. Get off me—it's not funny," she said, trying to move him again without success.

"In a way I think it's quite funny."

"Gordon, I want you off me now."

He shifted his knees slightly but it still hurt just as much.

"Come on, you're hurting me and scaring me."

"Two things you would never do to me, of course."

"Get off!" she screamed until he covered her mouth hard with his hand.

"Don't ever do that again or I'll hurt you a lot worse," he said, lowering his hand until it was around her throat, then keeping it there. "Learn to communicate softly. Whisper."

"Why are you doing this? Why do you want to hurt me?" she said softly but insistently. She kept asking him those questions, but he didn't answer for what seemed like several minutes (though she sometimes heard him muttering). Meanwhile, the pain in her arms was so intense she thought she'd pass out, and his hands were still around her neck, not hard, but in a perfect position to strangle her, so she felt she couldn't defy him again by screaming.

"Are you completely unaware of how much you've hurt me tonight?" he finally said.

"No, yes. I'm unaware, what did I do?

"What did I do? What did I do? Poor Alice hasn't a clue," he said, finally removing his hands from her neck but putting even more pressure on her arms.

"Jesus Christ, will you get off me?" she said, trying to move him and then starting to cry.

"That won't help you either. Your crying will only make things worse. Crying and screaming and all your emoting and manipulating won't help you anymore. No one will hear you anyway."

She remembered about the walls then and thought she might get hysterical.

"What did I do?" she said. "What did I say that hurt you? I'm sorry, I can't imagine what it was but I'm sorry, truly sorry."

"I'm sure you are . . . now."

"I don't understand what I did or why you won't tell me."

"What would be gained by my telling you?"

"So I could apologize."

"And what would be gained by that?"

She looked puzzled for a second and tried not to cry again.

"Do you think all you have to do in life is say a little perfunctory apology and then you can get everything the way you want it?"

"No," she said. "No I don't."

"Do you think that if someone you know killed your mother and then said to you, 'I'm sorry, I apologize,' you'd respond by saying 'OK, I understand, now we can be friends again'?"

"No, of course not." She was thinking that she had to keep talking to him, that it would increase her chances of nothing bad happening.

"So what can someone do if they make the mistake of hurting someone?" she said.

"The best thing they can do is not make the 'mistake' in the first place, *capice*?"

"Yes, I understand," she said, trying to look ashamed, hoping that might appease him. She was thinking that what hurt him must have to do with sex, but she'd been so high it was hard to remember it. She didn't think anything unusual happened, thought she'd faked her orgasm reasonably well, as usual. Maybe she didn't compliment him enough, but that was because the pot made her so quiet.

"Are you beginning to understand now?"

"Yes, but what can I do?

"Do you want to see something I brought with me?"

"Will it hurt me?"

"It could, if you force me to."

"Is it a gun? Is that it?"

"It's possible, isn't it?"

She could feel her heart beating faster. "Are you going to shoot me?"

"Anything's possible. It depends on how you behave."

"I'll do whatever you want. Just don't hurt me."

He seemed to be studying her face until she thought she might faint waiting for him to speak.

"I'm going to give you a second chance," he finally said.

"Thank you," she said softly.

"I'm going to make a Kierkegaardian leap of faith and give you another opportunity to live better, but you have to do exactly what I tell you."

"I'll do whatever you say."

He got up then and she tried not to moan, though her arms were throbbing. "Stay still, till I say you can move," he said, as he got off the bed. Despite the dark, he got dressed very quickly, as if he knew exactly where everything was. He even appeared to be tying his shoes in the dark. Then he stood up, grabbed her hand, and told her to get out of bed.

"Come on."

"Where are we going?

"Right here," he said, taking a few steps with her while he held her with one hand and turned on the bathroom light with the other. The sudden light was shocking and intolerably bright. For a moment she felt embarrassed to be naked in front of him. Now he would see how skinny her breasts were and the unfortunate tattoo on her bottom. She felt herself start to shake.

"What are you going to do?" she said.

"The question is what *you* are going to do. And the answer is: take a bath. That's not too difficult, is it? Go on, pull aside the shower curtain and turn on the bath. Come on, turn the faucet on more. You want this to end soon, don't you? Well, it can't end till it begins."

Her hands were shaking on the faucets making it difficult to adjust the temperature. First she made the water too cold, then too hot. It was as if her fingers had turned into centipedes. Finally, she thought she got it more or less right, probably too hot but still the best she could do, and then she turned on the faucets full force and waited while the water roared like she was roaring inside.

"All right, that's enough. Turn off the water and get in now, and while you're in there I want you to think about what a bath is."

"What it *is*?"

"What it means. Think about purification and the chance to emerge a new person."

She was lying in the tub now, instinctively covering her crotch. She felt she had to keep appeasing him no matter what he asked for because he appeared to have no conscience or empathy and if she didn't he might just kill her like a bug.

"Based on how aggressive you were in the bar I'd say you have a lot to purify."

She nodded, still trying not to cry.

"Look at me while I talk to you. You were attracted to me in the bar, weren't you? It was you who pursued me and made this night happen. Am I correct?"

"Yes."

"You saw my physique in the clothes I was wearing and you couldn't resist me. You saw me well, didn't you?"

"Yes, I did."

"How attracted to me were you?"

"Extremely. A lot."

"But that's not a good reason to walk up to someone and tempt them and then get in a car with someone you don't know and go to their home, is it?"

"No."

"And that's something you've done before, I'm sure. You use men like a drug, don't you, so you can feel better about yourself. But that's very bad behavior. And it's bad for the man, too, because you don't know him, just like you don't know me. You may think you do but you don't. And what happens when you don't know someone is that you can hurt them very easily."

She nodded. "Yes, I see that now."

"Now I want you to wash yourself with that bar of soap very thoroughly, including your private parts, especially your private parts. Go on, put the bar of soap inside your pussy and wash out every speck of me."

"Yes," she said. "I'm doing it."

"I'm going to keep watching you to make sure you do."

She started washing herself while he stared at her. She was in the water but felt like she was in a desert where the sun was shining directly on her. Then he took a step closer, till he was right next to the tub.

"You're not washing yourself vigorously enough."

"Sorry, I will," she said, doubling her speed.

"Put the soap inside yourself and scrub. Are you going to make me do it?"

"No, I'll do it," she said, washing harder.

He leaned over so he could see better (making her wish again that she hadn't shaved there), and she thought briefly of splashing him with the hot, soapy water and trying to escape. She knew what he was doing, getting rid of any sign of himself. It was probably why the sex was so conventional, and why he hadn't hit her—even after she screamed—so that everything would look consensual.

"Stop thinking," he hissed at her, making her shake again. "I can hear your thoughts and I don't like them. Just keep washing yourself."

"OK."

"Harder."

"It's starting to hurt."

"OK, stop," he said. Then he pulled the plug and the water began to drain. He didn't say anything as he continued to watch her with a nondescript expression.

How could she have made love to him an hour ago—someone with no human heart? And now, for that one terrible decision, she might die. It was because she was so lonely, and loneliness made her panic and make bad decisions. Her job was stupid, the men she met were stupid—she had no one, no beauty in her life. Maybe she was searching for beauty.

"What are you going to do with me?" she said.

"Don't worry. I always have a plan."

She started crying softly. She didn't want to but she couldn't help it.

"You really don't know where you are, do you?"

"No, how could I?" she said, recovering quickly. "I passed out in the car and then it was so dark and when I asked where I was you didn't tell me."

"No, I didn't. It's lucky for you you drank so much that you passed out. Lucky for you and in a way unlucky for me because I'd love to drink now, but I can't because I have to drive."

"I'll drive, if you want me to," she said hopefully.

"No," he said, laughing a little, "that would be difficult, given my plan for you."

"Why? What are you planning to do? Are you worried that I'll tell someone about this?"

"Should I be?"

"No, no. What would I tell them?"

"Exactly."

"I made the decision to sleep with you."

"How was the sex, by the way?"

"Fine."

"Fine?"

"Great. Probably the best sex I've had in years."

"In years?"

"Probably ever. It was the best sex I've ever had in my life by far, I admit it."

"Really? That's strange. And here I thought you were faking and lying the whole time and making a fool of me. You should be grateful to me then for that experience and for the lesson I had to teach you about consideration and purification."

"I am grateful," she said weakly.

"All right, now get out of the tub and dry yourself off. I'll be watching you every second, of course. Then you'll get dressed and we'll go."

"Where? Where are we going?"

"Ah, don't expect answers to every question, otherwise I *will* start thinking you're a little girl."

She dried herself quickly and looked at him indecisively, not knowing what to do with the towel.

"Put the towel back on the rack," he said, knowing that she hoped she could wear it.

"Oh. OK," she said, taking it off her body slowly.

"Are you still scared? Be honest."

He was weirdly complicated, insisting on the truth on one hand and extreme flattery on the other.

"No, yes. I'm just a little confused and anxious."

"Would it help if you prayed?"

"Excuse me?" she said. Then he opened a cabinet door, took some kind of bag and removed a gun that he was now pointing at her. She stared at him. She looked like she'd been electrocuted, he thought, her eyes almost popping out of her head, like Little Orphan Annie's.

"Don't shoot, don't, don't," she repeated, holding up a hand.

"Calm down and I won't. All right? Just calm down, *tout de suite.*"

"OK."

"There, that's better. Would you like to pray now, would that help?"

"Here? You want me to pray here?"

"Yes, right here, right now. Get on your knees and pray for what you want out loud, so I can hear you."

She felt herself shake, like a rattlesnake was inside her. When she got down on her knees, the tile felt cold and knifelike.

"Go on," he said, standing over her and still holding the gun with one hand and the bag behind his back with the other.

"Dear God, I pray . . ."

"Wait a minute. Hold the phone. Who's 'God'? I don't know any God. Do you? Does God come over to your apartment to visit you? Does God ever invite you to dinner or take you for a drive in the dark to the suburbs?"

"What should I say? How should I do it?"

"Pray to me, Gordon. At least you know I'm real."

"You want me to pray to you?"

"Yes."

"OK. Dear Gordon," she said in an uncertain voice, "I pray that you won't hurt me and will take me home now."

A flash went off, then another. She looked up and realized he had photographed her while she was praying. He put the camera behind his back in the bag he was holding and said, "Guess what? I've decided to grant most of your prayer. I won't hurt you if you continue to cooperate, *capice?*"

"Yes. I'll cooperate. Whatever you want."

"All right," he said, taking her by the hand into the bedroom, where he turned on an overhead light. "Get in your clothes now, *tout de suite.* And by the way, the picture looks like it will turn out well. Do you want to see it?"

She didn't say anything. She looked at the floor, where most of her clothes were in a tangle. She tried to move quickly but her legs felt sore and sluggish, as if uninterested in cooperating. When she finally put her shoes on she said, "You're not going to shoot me are you? You're not going to kill me?"

"I already shot you with a camera," he said, looking at her with an expression that was meant to feign shock. "How many times do you want me to shoot you? Can you tell me why you would think something like that? I thought we agreed nothing had happened and you weren't going to talk about it with anyone because there's nothing to talk about."

"I won't," she said.

He shut off the light and began leading her by the hand out the door, still holding the gun as they got in the car. "There's nothing for me to worry about," he said. "You don't know where I live, and by the way I don't live here."

"I didn't think so."

"I don't even live in this state."

"I also don't know your last name," she added.

"Guess what, you don't know my first name either."

A tremor passed through her but she said nothing.

"I, however, know your name, Susan L. Hunt, *and* where you live, as well."

"How?"

"While you were sleeping I took a piece of identification from your pocketbook. I'm going to have to keep that ID, I'm afraid."

"I'm not going to tell anyone anything ever. I just want to go home."

"And you will get home, eventually."

She repeated his words right after he said them, as if she didn't trust her understanding of them. She felt that she often didn't quite know what he meant, as if he were speaking in riddles or with some secret kind of irony she couldn't grasp. Then she wondered why they were still sitting in the car.

"Are you still wondering what else I have in my bag?"

"Yes," she said.

"Well, one of the things in it is a blindfold, which I'm going to have to put on you and tie a little on the tight side."

"But it's so dark anyway. I'll keep my eyes closed, I promise."

"Since it's so dark it won't make much difference then. And by the way, I recommend you keep your eyes closed while the blindfold's on. It will make it much easier for you."

"OK, whatever you want."

"I want you to promise me."

"I promise."

"Say, 'Dear Gordon, I promise to keep my eyes closed till you let me out.'"

"Dear Gordon, I promise to keep my eyes closed till you let me out."

She waited for him to say something else but he didn't. She could feel the car moving but couldn't tell how fast. The whole night kept surprising her, as if it were a car that constantly changed speeds. First things would happen very fast and then they'd go slow and stop and then go fast again.

She couldn't stop thinking about the gun, but how many times could she ask him not to shoot her, and what good would it do? She felt she'd spent her whole life trying to please and flatter men, always hoping they'd say things they never said. She closed her eyes, suddenly feeling tired, and saw her apartment, then her sister's face and her mother's, and then the trees across the street from the house she grew up in. Maybe there was some beauty in her life, after all. She opened her eyes then as if to see it better and kept them open the rest of the trip.

. . . .

"It's a shame," he said.

"What is?" she said, quickly, grateful that he was talking again (it seemed they'd driven an hour in silence), and hoping, somehow, that he'd put the gun away.

"That we got off on the wrong foot. That you hurt me. I think we could have become friends."

"Yes," she said softly.

"I've been thinking some more about poetic things and I have to change my conclusion. I think the most poetic thing in the world is friendship, just because you're not born into friendship like you are into your family. Because both people have to choose to be friends."

"I agree. I know what you mean . . . Gordon, where are you planning to drop me off?"

"It won't take you long to get home, don't worry. You have enough cash in your wallet. Trust in Gordon."

"I don't understand."

"I'm going to find a nice outdoor train stop for you. One where there aren't many cars or people, not at this time of night, and you'll get a train to Philly before too long."

"Can I take off my blindfold now?"

"I'm afraid you'll have to wait till I drop you off for that. By then I'll be long gone—just a stranger in the night, an eidolon. Oh, and by the way, I borrowed this car out of state. You'll never trace it."

"I won't try to. I never saw the license plate. Never saw it."

"No, I don't think you did. And I don't think you'll try to trace anything, either. I think you realize that you've learned a lot from me and that you'll behave differently in the future. And I don't think you'll ever forget me."

"No, I never will."

"In fact, you'll probably think about me a lot. And if you want to some time you can pray to me again."

A moment later she felt the car turn, felt it circling around slowly until it stopped. Then he reached across and opened the door.

"Well, I've got something to do now. I have to call a real friend of mine, my best friend in all the world. Now don't make a sound or take off your blindfold until I'm gone," he said sternly. Then he half helped, half pushed her out the door. She tried to stand still on the ground but fell down on something hard and gravelly. She heard his car back up and screech away into the night, reached behind herself and in ten seconds or so got the blindfold off. She stood up slowly and stared out at what she thought was his direction to be sure he was gone. Looking a little to the right she thought she saw the train stop, and despite knees that were probably bleeding, turned toward it and started to run, thinking, she didn't die, she didn't die after all, something completely different was happening.

He pulled away, staring hard and sitting upright, almost rigid, to see better. He didn't, wouldn't let himself think, till he was on the highway toward Philly. But it was not like the suburbs of New York, it was a series of little sleeping towns and townships and there were very few cars on the road. That was reassuring, but with less to watch it made him need to think more.

It was like driving away from a car wreck, like driving away from madness. And it *was* madness to try to help people like her, who couldn't be helped. Zombies, addicts—addicted to humiliation. One ended up being the fool, being the truly humiliated one and in his case having to live with the terror of being potentially punished, as well. At such times his mind became like a videotape reviewing the events of the evening over and over. Supposing someone were watching, what was the worst thing that had happened? He hadn't hit her, and God knows he hadn't raped her. He'd pulled a gun on her, that was true, but he'd only done it to make her listen to him. To get her attention. With zombie people like that, what other way was there? And she had listened, she had prayed and listened, so perhaps he'd made a difference.

He had to stay focused, not tilt like his mind was nothing more than a pinball machine. She'd reassured him over and over that she wouldn't tell anyone and he knew that was true. Besides, what could she say, what did she know? Nothing. Nothing to the ninth power. He merely had to concentrate on the image of Nothing. Being and Nothingness, as Sartre aptly called it. A patch of air above an empty lake. Nothing. "Nada y puis nada," as Hemingway called it. "The Night of the Living Dead," as Wes Craven called it, or was that another director?

It was time to focus on making himself feel better. Susan L. Hunt. (Love Hunt, he wondered?) was living in bad faith and maybe he had jolted her awake, made her move a little out of lockstep with the rest of the whores and zombies. But that wasn't the worst of crimes, was it? That wasn't even a crime at all.

Uncle Simon and Gene

They were just where they weren't supposed to be. It was clearly roped off, so how could the man not know it, Simon thought, digging his nails into the palms of his hands as he watched the two of them staring at the train layout. And what an example to set for his little boy, that was the worst part. It was just as if the man had stared into his little boy's shining blue eyes (who couldn't have been more than five) and said, When you want to do something, do it. Ignore the rules of your environment, forget the laws by which the meek of the world abide, and follow your pleasure wherever it may lead. If it leads you in a public museum to an area that's obviously roped off, ignore the ropes, pretend they don't exist. Indulge your appetite regardless of how you violate your surroundings—that's the important thing, sonny.

What would be next, Simon wondered? Would they lift off the glass lid that covered part of the exhibit? Would the man risk setting off the alarm just so his little boy could touch the trains, perhaps take the trains off their tracks and run them on the museum floor, and then when the whim struck them go somewhere else in the museum, the man putting the trains in his pockets so his little boy could play with them later amongst all his other stolen toys?

Would you believe it, he was touching the trains now, letting his little boy touch them, too, letting him pick them up in the air and examine them as if they were dollar toys and not miniature works of art that were part of the City Museum's special train exhibit.

The little boy was becoming talkative now. He was talking about cupolas, connecting rods, and hopper cars—a regular train fanatic he was and so naturally excited to see such an elaborate setup of model trains in such an intimate, clearly forbidden way. And to know that his father would break the rules of the museum (the laws of the city and state, too, for that matter) just to cater to his pleasure.

It was almost five o'clock and the museum was already emptying. From his position by the unoccupied trampoline Simon watched the man, who looked to be rather old to have such a young son, running his fingers through the boy's hair. Then he had an awful thought. How did he know that man was the boy's father? It seemed to him that from the time he'd watched them the man had touched the boy an excessive amount, couldn't, in fact, seem to keep his hands off him. Well, it wouldn't be the first time an arrogant pervert had paraded his conquest in a public place, Simon supposed, but he was damned if on his watch he was going to let it happen once he was sure what was what.

He decided to move a little closer to hear them better. Their words would give them away, he realized, especially the little boy's. Unless he was very well trained, for example, it was unlikely that the little boy would call the man daddy, although the man might actually be the child's father and *also* abusing him—that happened all the time, too. Museums were hardly able to safeguard children from such abusers. On the contrary, they were magnets for them, especially a place like the City Museum, which was *created* as a children's museum. Simon was staring openly at them now but the man (good-looking for his age, which was somewhere in his early to mid fifties—Simon's age) never noticed, never took his eyes or his hands off his young, adored treasure.

They were both talking now, man and little boy, quietly but animatedly, like coconspirators. They were acting out some kind of drama with the trains, giving them voices, names, and personalities and telling a story back and forth, ducking under more ropes from time to time as they added still more trains to their ever-expanding collection.

"Hey, you're wearing my shirt!" someone suddenly said, nearly yelling at the man, who turned away from his boy looking dumbfounded. It was Gene, Simon's thirteen-year-old nephew, who'd finally returned from his latest spontaneous adventure down a different hallway he'd insisted on seeing alone. Gene was still pointing at the man as he said, "I have a shirt just like that. You can only get them at Yosemite."

"A friend gave it to me," the man said, looking down at his chest and smiling. He was wearing a darkish-blue tee shirt with three yellow-and-red figures on it, part doll, part warriors, wearing masks, and the word *Yosemite* in gold letters on the bottom right. Simon hoped that would be the end of it (so did the little boy, who was tugging at the man's hand), but Gene, who was extroverted almost to the point of idiocy, at times, continued.

"Yo, were you there, man?" Gene said, falling into his hip-hop tone of voice.

"No, I hear it's really pretty."

"It was the best trip ever, man," Gene said, before lurching down the corridor toward Simon. Instinctively Simon turned slightly, so that if the man was watching him he would now see him in profile.

Well, it had not been that bad, nothing embarrassing at all, like when Gene once yelled at a man in a movie theater, "Hey, you're completely bald!" Always he said such things when you least expected it (though how *could* you expect it?) and always at movie theaters, museums, churches, or concert halls. It made Simon cringe and want to disappear (the baldness remark was particularly embarrassing because of his own retreating, thin gray hair). Another time, in a loud piercing voice, Gene had asked a woman with a big stomach if she was pregnant. That was terrible too. Though nothing like that had happened today, it would be more difficult now to continue his investigation of the man and boy. However, given their history, Gene would probably not be with him for very long. Gene never stayed and walked with him for long, even when he was a little boy. There was always something that caught his eye and made him run off somewhere leaving him alone. Today he would be left, he knew, in this strange museum where he'd have no choice but to watch other people he didn't know and see awful things of which the world had no end.

"Uncle Simon, did you see the shirt that man was wearing?"

"Yes, Gene, I did." I'm sure the whole world saw it, he said to himself with a smile. That was classic Gene. He embarrassed you or made you angry and a moment later made you smile. Even when he had his troubles in school, making jokes or just saying whatever outrageous thing came to his mind—while the teacher was talking, or worse still, during exams, when the room was supposed to be filled with a sacred quiet; Simon would smile when he heard about it. Of course, it was serious when Gene was sent to the principal's office and, then, usually sent home, and his father had to come get him and would call and tell him all about it an hour later. But even then, though he'd feel exasperation and the tragedy of it, he would also find it funny in spite of himself. He would suffer for that too. He would even feel ashamed, but damn, the boy did say some funny things, and when he put together the things he said with the expression that was probably on Gene's face and with the tone of voice with which he must have said them, it was impossible not to smile and usually laugh, as well.

Gene was supposed to be below average in intelligence and emotional maturity according to the tests. Not retarded or even very close to it, but supposedly well below average (though some of his remarks were extremely clever). He was not a good athlete either, so how else was he supposed to command attention in this world? At least this way he amused some people and stayed in their minds a little while. Small price to pay for a "personality disorder." It was as if as a very young boy he'd realized this about himself and begun even then to hone his bizarre comedic skills.

"Uncle Simon, where are we going now?" he said in his typically loud, innocent voice.

"Wherever you want to."

"They went through the ropes where you're not supposed to go," he said, pointing at the man and his lover boy.

"It's best not to imitate them, then, isn't it?"

"Uncle Simon, what about the tubes?" he asked, referring to the long maze of dark, interconnected crawl spaces and caves on the first floor.

"What about them?

"I want to crawl through them again."

"All right then," Simon said. Gene let out a yell and ran ahead of him. Simon shook his head and sighed.

Of all the things that had been said about Gene, and Simon had heard a lot, the one about him being below average in intelligence probably hurt the most. But why should he even take that judgment seriously? He was a mechanical engineer; he knew that, complicated as the machines he studied were, the mind was far more complicated and mysterious and no word could describe intelligence. Also, being childless and having lived alone all of his adult life, he'd achieved a certain objectivity and prided himself on that. He knew how little people knew—doctors and therapists probably least of all. He knew that at best people only knew a little bit about their own field (and that little bit was highly slanted according to their particular training and agenda) and almost nothing about anything else. The world was merely a constantly unfolding vaudeville show of misimpressions, misinformation, and mistakes. Slapstick with tragic consequences. That was why rules were so important to follow, why it was so wicked to break them, as the man and his lover/boy did. Because without rules there would be chaos—the very essence of evil.

They had reached the tubes and before he entered Gene let out a booming, Tarzanlike yodel, then yelled, "I'm Spider-man. I'm Worm-man!" Then he bent down like a monkey and entered the labyrinth, leaving Simon alone.

Simon looked around himself. Everywhere children were running and screaming, their parents running after them. This kind of frenzy was what people called family fun. Well, he had been spared that, at least, though he thought of himself as Gene's second father—especially given what little genuine interest his younger brother and his wife showed in the boy. Gene was an only child, and an accident. Though they wouldn't say it, they always regarded him as both an accident and a disappointment. Well, at least they met their financial obligations and loved him in a way. But what he had realized, especially these last few years, was that loving someone "in a way" was never enough and probably did as much damage as hating them.

What strange thoughts he was having. Maybe it was this so-called museum, a swollen, shabby, misshapen place—not like a museum at all but more like a set from *The Flintstones* gone amok. People wouldn't admit this, though, nor would they admit that it charged too much. That was because it was *supposed* to be a good place—a consensus had been reached, and once that happened people believed it *was* good, whether that something was a museum, a movie, a politician, or a restaurant. When you were in business, to have reached that positive consensus was the closest thing to heaven on earth. If the consensus had been reached in the media that a restaurant was good, for example, it could serve the vilest food in the Western world and people would brag about going there. In the same way, if a positive consensus had been reached about a politician he could destroy the economy, drop bombs on thousands of people, and endanger the world and continue to get re-elected by huge numbers. And teenage hit men (supposedly people more intelligent than Gene) from around the country would be standing in line waiting to enlist in his army to kill for him with proud smiles on their faces. Look at Hitler, to name only the first one who came to mind. Look at any of them.

That was one thing about Gene—the thoughts he did have were his own. He didn't read newspapers, didn't care what authority figures said. He was too uneducated to know what the consensus was and so always said what he truly thought. He had his innocence and honesty and that alone made him a genius compared to most people.

Simon shifted his feet uneasily. Gene had been in the tubes a long time and he was beginning to worry. He looked at his watch and decided that he'd wait two more minutes before crawling in after him. The tubes were supposed to be safe only because one assumed they were, but he had gone in there before and found all sorts of ledges and crevices where one could fall and be injured, or worse.

A minute and a half went by. Simon looked out across the floor and saw the man with the little boy approaching the huge indoor slide and sandboxes. The man was holding the little boy's hand. But he couldn't leave Gene now, could he, not when he wasn't *really* sure about the man's motive. Ah, life was so confusing. Nothing would happen for a very long time and then suddenly too many things happened at the same time. It was just the way it was with television. For days there would be nothing worth seeing and then there would be three shows he wanted to see all scheduled at the same time. He didn't like to see the man and his boy slip away, not with his dark suspicions about them. It pained him to potentially risk losing them again, but with Gene's nose for trouble and misfortune he really didn't have a choice.

So Simon bent down, never as easy as it used to be, and entered the tubes. It was darker than he'd remembered or imagined. Had there been some kind of power failure? He took several steps in the dark, then had to bend down again and start crawling to fit through the space. As soon as he started crawling he felt like a child. He could remember crawling like that when he was much younger than Gene, through a fun house, trying to catch up with his brothers. It seemed he was always trying to catch up with someone. First his father, who had such a big stride and always walked ahead of him down the sidewalk or on the beach. "Daddy," he would perpetually call out. "Daddy, wait for me." Then later, following after his brothers, even his younger brother (Gene's father), who was supposed to tag along after him.

Maybe that was why he never allowed himself to chase after women. He could not let himself be hurt that way, although the decision not to pursue them probably insured that he would end up alone, as he had, since he was never wildly attractive. But the way he chose was for the better, he was sure. For the most part he'd avoided humiliation, though it still seemed he was always watching others, as he'd watched the man and boy earlier in the museum, and then followed after them, and as he was now once again following after Gene.

He had to shift to his side and swore softly as he crawled over a rock-like protuberance that dug into his side. Below him to his left, separated only by a thin mesh screen, was a dimly illuminated pool where thick fish swam. Did they have teeth?

"Gene," Simon began calling. "Gene, where are you?" he said, almost yelling himself now.

He stayed completely still, as if that would help him hear better. Of course, one didn't need to do that to hear Gene, who'd never said anything softly in his life. Yet he waited, counted to ten, but heard nothing. Then he started crawling furiously through the winding tubes, feeling like a laboratory rat in a maze.

"Gene, Gene where are you?" he yelled. He saw again in his mind's eye the few awful seconds when Gene was seven and walking with him, then suddenly bolted and ran into the street, where a car hit him almost immediately (fortunately the car wasn't going fast and Gene "got off" with just a broken leg). Those seconds, the worst of his life, had never left him completely. In moments of anxiety they'd reappear as vivid as paintings in a preternaturally bright museum.

"Gene, can you hear me? It's Simon." He crawled some more. "Gene?"

"Yo, Uncle Simon. I'm in a cave."

Simon looked around himself wildly. It was incredible that this "museum" charged so much money for people to crawl through places as dark and dangerous as this. Finally, twenty feet and seven rock steps below him, he saw Gene smiling inside one of the caves—saw his incredibly white teeth first—as white as stars, and then his great dark eyes somehow also shining, and wanted to hug him though he hadn't done that in years. Only shook his hand now because Gene wanted it that way.

"Gene, why didn't you answer me?"

"I didn't hear you, Uncle Simon. Not until the last time. I've just been hanging in this cave," he said, still smiling ear to ear.

For a moment Simon thought of bats hanging in the cave, wouldn't put it past this place if it did have real bats or worse.

"I was worried about you."

"This cave is cool because no one knows about it. No one's been in it but me the whole time."

"But I didn't know about it either and I was worried when I couldn't find you."

"But you did find me, Uncle Simon."

Simon smiled.

"Yes, you're right. I did."

"Do you want to sit in the cave next to me?"

It would mean bending down again like a monkey, but breathing heavily and coughing once or twice, he sat next to Gene.

"The cave is cool, right?"

"Yes, the cave is cool," he said. It was kind of fun sitting in it now, where there was just enough space for the two of them.

"I can see lots of legs of people but they can't see me."

"The cool cave is well hidden," Simon said.

"Yes, and besides, legs don't have eyes," Gene said, making them both laugh. "They had caves like this in Yosemite, Uncle Simon."

"Really?"

"Yes, really cool caves."

Gene had been in Yosemite a mere three weeks before on a family vacation. Gene's father loved mountains. He was the rugged brother in the family, and he'd taken Gene mountain climbing. Simon had worried every day that they were gone, but Gene had returned talking of little else these last weeks. He loved doing things with his father, of course. Although he'd probably done more things with his uncle, he naturally treasured doing things with his father. That was inevitable.

"That man in the Yosemite shirt," Simon said suddenly. "What did you think of him?"

"He just walked by me."

"While you were in the cave?"

"Yes."

"How could you tell?"

"I could hear him talking to his son."

So the man had taken his little boy into the heart of darkness too.

"How long ago did you see them?"

"Just a couple of minutes before you found me."

Simon fought an urge to bolt after them. But he wouldn't know where to go or how to find them. Two minutes were an eternity in the darkness of the tubes.

"What were they talking about, do you remember?"

"Just laughing a lot and having fun."

"Are you sure it was them? Did you hear the boy call him 'Daddy'?"

"Yes, he called him 'Daddy' and 'Dad' the whole time."

Simon inhaled deeply.

"What did you think of the man?" Simon said. "Did you like him?"

"Yes. I think he's a really cool dad."

"You're probably right, Gene, you're probably right. You usually are about people. More right than me, I've noticed."

"Why is that Uncle Simon?"

"I don't know. I haven't figured out the answer to that yet."

Gene nodded, then for some reason stopped talking just when Simon would have loved to hear some of his banter, even at its silliest. But Gene continued to smile as he stared out into the half-light, filled with giggles and running feet.

Simon couldn't think of anything to say either. A feeling of sadness and fatigue was slowly invading him.

So, in all likelihood, he had been wrong about the man and boy. But, if he was honest with himself, this kind of thing had happened before. He was, if not exactly paranoid, an alarmist, filled with ominous suppositions and theories about people if they did not behave a certain way. And he had been this way all his life, or all his adult life. He tried to think back and get a picture of himself in his adolescent years, when it seemed to him he was mostly trusting. Innocent was perhaps the better word. But, whatever, he had begun by thinking of life as innocent until proven guilty, and even that would be an understatement. He had really begun by assuming that people were honest and good and meant what they said. He had begun by being like Gene. When you were Gene's age, no matter what your supposed intelligence, you didn't think there was a cave inside people's hearts because there was no cave inside your own.

What had happened to him then? Was it because the first girl he'd tried to love when he was sixteen lied to him, and the next one, whom he did love at eighteen, left him for someone else? Not a great beginning, to be sure, but something that happens to millions of men, and of course the quirks in his personality had a lot to do with it, too (that's what love affairs were, essentially, the interactions of quirks and wounds).

The astonishing thing, though, was how easily he had become discouraged, assuming he was cursed for life because of two early failures. How quickly he had gone to his cave. There was no answer, or no easy one for that. It was odd. You begin with a disease and then spend the rest of your life trying to master it or at least identify it. The therapists tried to help but they were too preoccupied with lining their pockets. It got in the way, as money always did.

Ah, what a silly, useless thing for him to think about now in his fifties, to be sitting in a cave still remembering the hair and smiles and even the smell of those long-ago girls.

"Gene, has the cat got your tongue?"

"No, Uncle Simon."

"Has the cave got your tongue, then?"

Gene laughed and Simon breathed more easily.

"Yo, that was funny. Has the cave got your tongue!"

"Maybe I should have been a comedian?"

"You are a comedian, Uncle Simon."

"It's nice to hear you laugh, but tell me, are we going to spend the rest of our lives in this cave, 'cause if we are I want to make some home improvements."

"What would you want to improve?"

"I'd like to get some pillows so we could lie back and, for that matter, an entire mattress would be nice."

"What else, Uncle Simon?"

"Then we could use a hot plate."

"What's a hot plate?"

"OK, how about a microwave. A kind of cordless microwave so we could cook food when we got hungry."

"What 'bout a refrigerator too?"

"A refrigerator would be nice too. And then we could use some kind of telescope that could see in the dark so we could tell what's around us. We'd have to invent that so we could watch other people and have some entertainment."

"I'm not smart enough to invent that."

"You're plenty smart," Simon said, giving Gene's hand a squeeze. "You're the smartest person I know."

He didn't look at him, then, though he half wanted to. He was somehow afraid of seeing his face and of Gene seeing his. They fell silent again but this time he decided he wouldn't rush Gene, that it wasn't really so bad what they were doing, sitting in the cave together. He could already imagine the rest anyway, the way it would end. The museum's closing bells would ring, lights would flash and dim, announcements would be made. Gene would move ahead of him running down the hallway. His father would be late as he always was, and Simon would worry every minute as he looked out the window of the museum lobby waiting for his station wagon to pull up.

When his father would finally arrive, Gene would get very excited. He would jump up and down and yell like Tarzan. He would run toward the car and he, Simon, would be left alone, would maybe say a word or two to his brother, trying to cover up his little hurt and envy, or else just wave and smile from a distance, as he had done so many times. Though it was only late afternoon in the summer, it would somehow seem dark outside. Later he would eat out, as he often did, to postpone facing his apartment. He would have a general anxiety about the dark and of being visited in his mind again by those long-ago girls. No, it was nothing to hurry up for. Not at all.

"Your father will be here soon, Gene. Won't that be exciting?"

"Yes, Uncle Simon, it will."

"Let's get up and go then, come on, or I'm afraid we'll be late."

Gene looked surprised, almost sad, to have his peace interrupted but stood up without any more discussion.

"You'd better lead the way out of here," Simon said. "Can you do that?"

"Sure, you should have seen me climbing at Yosemite."

"I'll settle for you getting us out of here safe and sound."

"No problem," he said, crawling ahead of him. "Yo, watch me!"

"Just don't go too fast. I'm an old man you know."

And so they crawled through the tubing and the caves, with all their snakelike turns. When they stepped out the bells were ringing and the light seemed as strong as the sun.

"The light is blinding," Simon said.

"I know. It's like the sun, Uncle Simon."

CRUISE

"I'll go first then, Captain, that's what you want, isn't it?" Rider said yes, though he'd never said he'd wanted him to go first, hadn't even been asked the question, and here was Anderson already seizing it from him. Wasn't that the way things always were, someone seizing something then pretending they weren't interested in what they'd just taken. All the more reason not to get too attached to things. That was why the second he saw the ad for the cruise in the newspaper he knew he'd take it, improbable though it was for him, of all people, to go. He simply saw an image of himself leaving everything behind him forever and fell in love with the image and its impeccable irony.

Anderson was barely audible above the competing sounds of the ship and sea, and Rider asked him to speak louder. His story still seemed to be in the preamble stage as far as Rider could tell. It was odd how Anderson did things, even odder that they were apparently going to go through with "the game," as Anderson called it, although they'd only known each other a few days.

They'd met because they were seated next to each other in the ship's dining room. There was no grand stroke of fate in that, Rider didn't think, especially since, as they each admitted later, there was no one else at the table even remotely interesting. Anderson struck him as a man who had suffered but still had a sense of humor and was still somewhat charming, which Rider found strangely touching. Later they met again at the shuffle-board tournament and quietly mocked it together. That night after dinner they drank in the bar, making fun of the whole cruise, which of course was steeped in absurdity, and then ridiculed themselves for taking it. It was in that spirit of self-mockery and margaritas that Anderson proposed the game. Already they'd fallen into the habit of talking quite openly with one another—or at least Anderson had.

"You can tell me anything and I wouldn't bat an eye," Anderson said, on their second night of drinking, and Rider said the same thing. Good, Anderson had said, because he had a bad conscience over something he really wanted to tell him about. Feel free to, Rider had said, assuring him he was a good listener. That's essentially what the game was, talking and listening, its object simply being to tell each other the worst thing they'd ever done—a clean confessional at sea. They'd decided to play it on the lower deck at midnight. Not bad as a final gesture, Rider thought to himself, with a grim smile. Anderson said it would be cleansing for both of them and fun, too, if they kept their humor. Anderson didn't even seem like a man who had done a worst thing. He was overweight and laughed a lot, with a beard that, despite being mostly black (and despite his dark intensely focused eyes, which almost matched Rider's own), still made him look more like Santa Claus than the devil. Rider pictured evil men as generally being thin and sensitive, tortured men as also being on the thin side, as he was. Certainly evil men didn't laugh a lot, as Anderson was doing now:

"You sure you're up for this, Captain?"

"Totally up, totally ready," Rider said, forcing a laugh himself, and forcing himself to pay attention, though he was not at all confident that he could actually listen to Anderson's story. How could he be, with what he was considering?

"Do you mind stories about women?"

"What else is there to talk about?" Rider said, and they both laughed. "I just lost my last lover so I'm sure I'll understand," Rider added, swallowing some of his drink. Anderson was clearly ahead of him drinkwise, but in spite of everything, he was afraid to catch up.

"It's strange about women, how once they're past forty-five they become more like us, while we get more like them. Or haven't you noticed? Maybe you're too young to notice, how old are you?"

"I'm twenty-seven," Rider said, lowering his age by five years.

"So you're even younger than I thought. I have the habit of thinking everyone else is older than they are and that I alone am younger than I really am. Anyway, what I mean is women get more aggressive sexually and more assertive in general while men become less so once we hit fifty. Instead we become more emotional and weepy. At a certain point I think the genders meet and form a kind of third sex. The point is, until I met Francine I believed I was following that pattern and was a new member of that third sex who had completely reversed his old ways."

"Which were?"

"I don't follow," Anderson said.

"What were your old ways?"

"To dominate, of course. To have as much power and control as possible in every situation, especially in bed. Wasn't that ever the way it was with you? Or maybe I'm way off base here. Sometimes I project stuff from my own life onto people simply because I think . . . well, simply because I do.

"Anyway, about my old ways with women all you need to know is that there was the usual amount of blindness and bungling—a wife, a divorce, some girlfriends, some one-night stands, and whatever you'd call the vast in-between. Let's see, what else? There were a few stabs at having children, though only one was born . . . who's quite a successful architect. If you ever asked him I think he'd say I was a good father or at least a nice man."

Rider made a noise to show he was impressed, and Anderson smiled briefly before speaking again.

"Then one final torturous love affair that ended with my thinking that I'd had enough. That I didn't want another woman—ever. I began to get fatter then as the months went by—swollen looking, like I am now. It was like all the hurts I'd been carrying around inside me had spread out on my body. But then, despite all that, eventually the old itch for them came back and I started answering singles ads again. After a few crummy ones I met Francine at a bar in Center City. Have you ever known someone who's both pretty and homely at the same time? I hadn't until I met Francine. She had natural platinum blond hair and pretty green eyes but her nose was too big, her lips too small. Swollen nose, shrunken lips, I remember thinking in spite of myself and the new sensitive-type man I thought I'd finally evolved into. It was the same with her body, which also had a swollen quality like . . . well, like mine."

Rider laughed, a little too loudly he thought, but Anderson continued, apparently without noticing.

"Homely or pretty, pretty or homely, I remember thinking throughout our drinks. It was like a tug of war in my head. Later I realized that there would be moments when she would be pretty and moments when she wouldn't. That's what happens when women are ambiguously pretty."

"To say nothing of men."

"Yes, of course it applies to us too," Anderson said. "There were other paradoxes. She had a soft, tentative voice, the most vulnerable voice I've ever heard, touching and arousing, but at the same time it was hard for her to talk and she often spoke or mumbled in an ungrammatical and confusing way. I'll need a hearing aid and a translator to understand this one, I thought. It was another tug of war, another stalemate. Finally my hand landed on her thigh, we started kissing, and I was instantly erect, something that hadn't been happening a lot lately. Well, I guess the tie is broken, I thought. She seemed to heat up right away too. After a few minutes she said, 'Let's go back to your place.' When we got there we continued making out before we even took our coats off.

"In bed, she was by far the noisiest woman I'd ever been with--as if she were making up for how quiet she was otherwise. It was like an air raid had gone off, and not just when she came but during the whole time. So noisy that she got me 'off message' at times, by making me worry that despite my thick walls my neighbors would think a homicide was being committed and call the police, who would suddenly burst into my room shooting first and asking questions later. Then as soon as our orgasms were over she was quiet again. Disappointingly so."

"When you might have expected to collect your compliment," Rider said.

"Yes, despite my hints, it was always that way. Maybe it was her way of spiting me."

"Still, on balance it sounds like a Playboy fantasy to me," Rider said. "Woman Who Has Nothing to Say Does All Her Talking in Bed."

"Yes, there was an element of that. It might have been like that if I could have controlled myself."

"Oh? How so?"

"I mean that I was at least ten years older than her. I should have realized what I was dealing with, especially as the details about her life began to trickle in. Her sexual abuse as a child from her uncle, her physical abuse from her ex-husband, her brief stays in various psychiatric wards. Part of me did realize it, of course, but I still couldn't seem to resist. It was like that part of me I'd thought had died out in my thirties was back stronger than ever. Already by the end of the first night she was addressing me as 'master.'"

So it's another slave story, Rider thought, as Anderson began to supply more details. It seemed men, particularly men he was interested in one way or another, were always telling him stories like that which he didn't want to hear, yet he'd listen anyway, which made him a kind of slave too, didn't it? I should just die now to avoid hearing it, he thought, looking up for a moment at the rash of stars. Years ago he used to believe they had ultimate control over people's fate. Now they were all out but it meant nothing, of course, the stars being silent as they always were.

He had thought the cruise would be the ideal place to do it—to die among the people he could never live with—the straight world, which had treated him like an alien all his life. The irony was airtight and Rider considered himself an irony connoisseur. But the idea that Anderson would be his last witness was disturbing on several levels. That this monologue by an aging, quasi-sadistic egotist should be the last speech he'd ever hear was too depressing. Even now Anderson had more than a trace of a smile as he continued to describe Francine servicing him and waiting on him. He had expected more from Anderson too—but wasn't that the way things always were? It was like a law of human physics—in the process of observing people they disappointed you. He remembered some years before Neal, his last lover, had stabbed him in the back, going to the apartment of a man named Al, who he'd met at a music-lover's club in Boston, a man who was going to play the piano for him. He didn't know if anything sexual was going to happen but he knew they were friends and he admired and respected him and looked forward to his piano playing. When he got to his music room he saw photographs of Al's female conquests draped over his piano. Obviously Al wanted him to comment on how beautiful they were, and of course he didn't. Very disappointing. He'd had high hopes for him, at least as a friend, and now this Al syndrome was happening again with Anderson.

"In the first few weeks I used to occasionally go out to eat with her," Anderson was saying (and Rider, in spite of himself, began to listen again), "and once even to a movie, but increasingly I didn't want to be seen with her in public. Even now I'm not sure why. I thought it was simply because I'd finally decided she was homely. I'm ashamed to say that to you now, but we agreed the whole point was to be brutally, completely honest. Am I right?"

"Go on," said Rider.

"Other times I thought it was because of the guilt I felt about how I treated her. Anyway, we began meeting exclusively for sex. A few times she mentioned that she'd like to go to a movie or at least leave the apartment for some reason other than to bring me food, but I reminded her, with a smile on my face, that it wasn't up to her to make decisions. Then she'd quickly say 'You're right' or 'I know, master,' and the matter was dropped."

"This slave business," Rider said, lowering his voice as a young couple holding hands passed by, "I'm not sure I understand. How serious was it?"

Anderson looked away from him at the water. "It was something we joked about at times—though during sex we carried out our roles with complete seriousness. Don't get me wrong, I never hurt her physically. I never enjoyed that or condoned that in bed. Almost every time I'd ask her if certain things were hurting and she'd say one way or another and if it was hurting her I'd stop. Also I'd ask her, you know, if she enjoyed our roles and she'd say yes, simply and convincingly. 'Why?' I would sometimes ask. 'I like a strong man,' she would say, or 'I love pleasing you.'"

"This is not a very uplifting story," Rider said, "but on the other hand, since she chose to act that way and told you she enjoyed it, I don't really see where the sin is."

"Wait, I'll tell you," Anderson said. "You see, things changed. She began writing me long, romantic love letters. Though she was poor she also began buying me gifts. Plants and flowers and crystals with perfumed cards attached.

"'We could have did more last night,' she wrote in one of her letters. 'You could have held me a little afterwards . . . why don't you ever want to hold me or have me stay over? Where is this relationship going?'

"I never answered with a letter of my own but in bed that night I brought it up.

"'I read your letter,'" I said. She looked away with an embarrassed smile. She was short, barely the height of a child, and she looked at that moment just like a child caught stealing the proverbial cookie from the cookie jar. I told her the things she said in her letter were nice but I didn't understand her asking about what kind of relationship we had. Her face turned beet red then.

"'I thought I was clear about that,' I continued. 'We're having a sexual relationship, Francine, in which we each have our roles. I thought we both understood that.'

"'But you said you loved me,' she blurted, suddenly staring at me with pathetically sincere blue eyes. She was alluding to something I'd said during sex a month or two before, near the beginning of our relationship, something I'd completely forgotten but which I now remembered vividly.

"'Yes, I did say that. And at the moment I said it I meant it.'

"Finally her eyes softened until something like a smile was back on her face. But somehow I couldn't leave it like that.

"'It was an expression of pleasure that I was feeling at the moment while we were having sex . . .'

"The look of profound unhappiness replaced the hopeful smile like a shade drawn over her face. That wouldn't do either.

"'Francine, I do love you . . . in my own way.' I added.

"With that uneasy compromise we were able to drop it for a while, but I knew it wouldn't go away. Just a second," Anderson said, as he stopped a waiter carrying a tray of complimentary piña coladas and took one for each of them.

"I knew I was in a mess," Anderson said as he swallowed his drink. "I was doing these rather extreme physical and psychological things with her for an hour or so and then after it ended I'd apologize, seeking reassurance that she really wanted it, really enjoyed it. And even though I always got that reassurance I never fully believed it, especially after the love letters started coming.

"'Why do I do it?' I'd ask myself. 'I do it because I can do it,' I'd answer, 'and also because it's simply irresistible to do.' But I knew I had to do something to change things so I began answering other ads, going out on dates with other women, though I also continued meeting Francine for our sessions. For a while things were in a holding pattern. I continued doing ever more bizarre things with Francine. Meanwhile she continued to do more things for me out of bed, too. To shop and cook for me and meet me at the airport when I returned from business trips, though I still felt uncomfortable walking through the airport with her. By the way, do you also travel a lot in your work?"

"Me?" Rider said, poking himself in his chest with his index finger. "I'm basically just a bookkeeper, though I'll answer to the word accountant. I picked a job where my emotions wouldn't be involved, where only a small part of my brain would be . . . taxed, you might say. Otherwise, there's too much stress and disappointment. And no, I don't travel for my job either."

Anderson laughed, finished his drink, then got them two more. "When my car broke down," he said, handing Rider his drink, "she drove me even more. She drove me for my root canal and then trips to a different suburb to see my accountant. Too bad I didn't know you then, I'd have thrown my business your way. The love letters continued also, all about the power of unconditional love and about our future. It was during this time that I found out about her uncle and her ex-husband, who never sent her any money, although one of his teenage sons still lived with her."

Anderson paused while a big-bosomed redhead in a clinging pink tee shirt walked by. He smiled at Rider and they each took a big swallow from their new drinks.

"You see," Anderson said, "it's not that I didn't care about her. I was even touched by her at times. Actually, I'd fallen into the habit during the apology segment of our sessions of trying to pump up her self-esteem, so it was natural that I'd ask her about why hers was so low. When she told me about her uncle she said, 'I feel like the worst thing has already happened to me, that nothing else could ever be as bad.' I also found out that for the last five years she'd been on antidepressants, which she got from some kind of doctor she'd been seeing.

"'Do you tell him about the things we do?' I asked in a worried tone. "She shook her head no, back and forth like a pendulum. 'No, that's personal,' she said.

"'Good,' I said, 'let's keep it that way.'"

"How exactly did you try to pump up her self-esteem?" Rider asked, with a tinge of sarcasm.

"I told her she was a passionate, highly emotional woman who had a lot to give. I told her that if she acted important people would treat her that way. I urged her to get a lawyer, too, and to hound her ex-husband for money (some of which she finally got) and to demand more than the crummy wages they paid her at the floral shop where she worked. She was an incurable lover of plants and flowers."

"And did she get the raise?"

"She got the raise."

"So you did do some good for her life."

"Yes, in those limited areas, but meanwhile I was dating other women and finally started sleeping with one—in a very conventional way—that I was mildly attracted to. My point is I still didn't give up Francine when I should have."

Anderson put his glass down on the small table by their chairs. "'I do it because I can do it' became my mantra, my explanation for everything I did with her. It never occurred to me that I did it because she let me do it. That included my cheating on her. I didn't want to tell Francine about my other girlfriend but I didn't want to deceive her either. Of course what I really wanted was her permission to do what I was doing. One night in bed . . ."

"Where else?" Rider said.

"Yes, where else, I told her that she had to live by different rules than me. One of those rules was that she could never ask me about other women.

"'Is there somebody else?' she said with that comically sincere expression back in her eyes.

"'Stop right there. Don't you see you're already breaking the rule?' I said, and she mumbled that she was sorry.

"I might have left it at that."

"But you didn't."

"No, I didn't. Instead I brought it up the next two times we met, and on the last time I finally told her I was sleeping with someone else.

" 'I knew it anyway,' she said softly.

" 'Are you OK?' I asked.

" 'I love you unconditionally,' she said, saying her favorite word again more loudly than usual. She was biting her lip a little but other than that looked all right.

" 'Thank you for accepting me,' I said. After we had sex she fixed me a snack and I still didn't notice any difference in her. She spoke about the power of love again. I told her she could stay over, thinking it would make her happy, and she did. I remember that I did hold her that night, and that it felt strangely peaceful. I vaguely wondered why I hadn't done it more often. When she left the next morning I really didn't think anything was wrong. But, of course, something was wrong. Before she left my place she'd swallowed a lot of her new pills, began driving on the wrong side of the road, and ultimately smashed up her car. Miraculously she wasn't badly hurt but she was arrested and taken to the hospital where her stomach was pumped. Then she was placed in a psychiatric ward where she eventually called me. 'I just couldn't see the point of going on,' she said.

"She called me a couple of other times from the hospital. After each call I wondered if she was still alive and hadn't really died in between calls. One night I dreamed that she had died and that it was her ghost talking to me on the phone. The next morning I managed to switch my vacation time and booked myself on this fabulous cruise."

"Just in the nick of time," Rider said, drawing a hard look from Anderson.

"Obviously you disapprove of that too, of my taking the cruise. But remember, this is me at my absolute worst, which is what we promised to reveal to each other."

Rider stared back at him, catching Anderson's eye before looking away from him. He watched a man walk by and then a woman, noticed the different sounds their shoes made on the deck. The man was carrying a drink, the woman her purse. There was some nauseating pseudo-Caribbean waltz whose name he couldn't remember being played by a few musicians on the deck above. Then he realized that the ocean wasn't roaring anymore and wondered if he had just gotten used to its sound.

"So I'm awaiting your verdict," Anderson said. "What do you think of all this? Should I walk the plank right now for what I did?"

"It's not a pretty story, is it?" Rider said, finishing his drink.

Anderson shook his head. He looked like an old little boy.

"It's disappointing," Rider said. "But I often find myself disappointed with people, did I already say that to you? It's odd how we allow ourselves to be disappointed so many times. You'd think we'd learn."

"What was it that you expected?"

"I remember once I went to Cape Cod with a friend, a male friend named Jay. This was a long time ago; I was in my early twenties. My friend was young and smart and full of energy. He was even valedictorian of his graduating class, or so he told me. I believed him because he had a tremendous ability to convince people of things, like you had with Francine, and so I believed him. We'd met at a record store where we were working in the summer. The kind of job recent college graduates did before grad school or setting out on a career. Soon we began pining for the beach and talking about it a lot at work. People in Boston, where I lived then, went to the Cape the way Philadelphians go to the shore . . ."

"Yes I know," Anderson said.

"And so we went to Hyannisport, me and my friend Jay, who I had such high hopes for."

"What kind of hopes?"

"Just hopes for a friend you could trust. I hadn't known everything about him, of course, but I had hopes and belief in a general way that he wanted the same kind of thing from life and from . . ."

"You."

"Yes, from me. That he expected a certain code of behavior, of character, that didn't even need to be discussed because it was understood."

"You certainly thought about this friend a lot."

"I always take people seriously, probably to a fault."

"And so what happened?"

"And so we found a motel and went to the beach and had a magical time swimming and playing Frisbee and laughing—it seemed like we laughed all day. And then we went to a steak house and it just continued. I don't think I'd ever had as much fun as I did that day and to cap it off with some good steaks . . ."

"Which we certainly haven't gotten here," Anderson said.

"No, hardly. But to have those kinds of steaks when you're so young and don't normally eat that way and then with our dessert we had a glass of champagne, which inspired us to buy a case of beer later that we took back and drank at the motel."

"You were young," Anderson said.

"Yes, I was young. And after this most perfect, this happiest day and night of my life I woke up in the morning and discovered that Jay, the valedictorian, had driven away in his car and taken all of my money."

"Really?"

"Yes, I found out at work two days later that he'd already given notice. He was leaving Boston for Oregon, where he was going to live."

"So he left for Oregon with a few hundred extra dollars courtesy of your pants pocket."

"He left the day after he robbed me. I'm sure he planned the whole thing."

"That stinks. That's really dreadful. But it sounds like the worst thing someone ever did to you, not the worst thing you ever did. Aren't you still going to finish the game and tell me what that is?"

"It *was* the worst thing I ever did. It's like the worst things I do are the things I let others do to me."

"You've lost me."

"Because part of me knew he would rob me. I may have even heard it while it was going on but I let him do it anyway."

"I don't understand."

"No, you don't."

"You speak as if there was something between you two. I mean . . ."

"You said I could tell you anything. Well, now I have."

"So . . . what I'm thinking is . . .."

"That I'm gay and you're right. Think about it. I never told you I wasn't."

"That's true."

"As for my valedictorian, he . . ."

"Wasn't."

"I don't know about that. I've thought about it a lot. Once someone lies to you, once someone misrepresents himself, you can never really be sure of anything about him. I don't know how thoroughly he planned it. It could have been a spur of the moment thing when he woke up that morning and saw me asleep and my pants on the floor or before we ever stepped in his car to go to the Cape or at any point in between. I know that that night I gave myself to him totally, let him do and get whatever he wanted from me physically and emotionally, and I was so happy surrendering to him (I would never surrender like that again to anyone) that it didn't bother me that he barely touched me or gave a thought to physically satisfying me."

"Possibly because he wasn't gay."

"Possibly . . . or else because he couldn't deal with it. But I'm sensing from your tone that this story is upsetting you, making you uncomfortable, or maybe it's just that I told you I'm gay."

"Not at all," Anderson said, waving his hand dismissively.

"I mean you haven't looked me in the eye once since I told you."

"I rarely look people in the eye."

"And the expression on your face, your whole tone of voice."

"If anything, I'm feeling that you disapprove of me . . . profoundly . . . that the story I told you understandably disgusted you and that you think of me as some kind of monster who you could never be friends with."

"I wouldn't say 'monster.'"

"What would you say?"

"I would say, I'd admit I thought you were different based on our earlier meetings. I'll admit that."

"So there you are disapproving of me while copping out on the game by telling me the worst thing that ever happened to you instead of the worst thing you ever did, like you were supposed to."

"But I also told you I'm gay. From your point of view isn't *that* the worst thing?"

Anderson sat up straight in his chair. "That's ridiculous. That's bullshit. You don't have any reason to say that to me, any more than if I said what really disappointed you about my story is that I turned out to be straight."

"Is this the part where we get into a fight on the deck so someone can yell 'man overboard!'?" Rider said.

Anderson didn't say anything but continued looking at him.

"You would probably win since as a faggot I'd surely turn out to be a hysterical and inept fighter. Still, I'm probably a good twenty years younger than you."

"We haven't established your age. You've been too vain to really tell me."

"You're a fine one to talk about vanity. You tortured some pathetic creature just so you could feel good about yourself sexually one last time. And then telling me all this sex stuff full of such great remorse but really full of not-so-subtle bragging about how good you are in bed, and you want reassurance from me?"

Anderson's face reddened and Rider felt he should stop but for some reason couldn't. "You get on this cruise to do penance but what you really want is for the first person you meet to hear your story and forgive you. Then it will be on to new conquests, new lies, new . . ."

"So what is it *you* want? Why are you even on this boat? Aren't there any gay cruises on the ocean these days? This is a straight person's singles cruise and since you've spent most of your time with me, what is it that you really want?"

"It isn't what you're suggesting, I can definitely assure you of that," Rider said, breathing hard. He could feel his heart beating. "Besides, it was you who was pursuing *me*, you who wanted to play the game and who did all the talking."

"Careful, fellah," Anderson said, pounding his fist on the table.

Rider's face whitened. "I'm leaving," he said, getting up from his chair and immediately feeling tremendously dizzy.

Anderson got up from his chair too. "Yes, it's better if we don't meet again," he said, but before he could continue Rider had turned his back and walked away.

Anderson swore to himself, felt himself turning an intense, insane red, brighter than he'd ever been, as if his face had been the subject of a child's fierce drawing. He felt he had to shield it from the other passengers as he walked mad and dizzy down the deck to his cabin.

Once in his room he punched his mattress twice, then his pillow several times in a row. He should have hit that little pussy; he should never have let him say all those awful things about him. Incredible how Rider, how people in general, couldn't face the truth about themselves or other people, though in each case they thought they wanted to.

When he stopped hitting he lay down on his bed breathing hard and feeling a strange kind of sadness. He looked at the round little ship's clock on his bedside table, thought of the idiots he'd have to face at lunch tomorrow and thought then that some of the things Rider said were true. But how could he say them, how could he know? And why did he tell Rider so much about himself in the first place? Part of him must have wanted Rider to hate him, but why? Anderson felt old then, older than he'd ever felt, and closed his eyes trying to hear the ocean. Instead he started thinking about his mother. He could still see in his mind's eye her hugging him as a child so close to her heart, and the thought of that made tears spill from his still-shut eyes, which he allowed to trickle freely down his face.

* * * * * * * * * *

Rider walked at a fast clip still holding his drink until he reached the back deck. The water roared white and black beneath him. How absurd that even now when he'd thought it would be the end, he was still reviewing and answering Anderson's questions, just as throughout his life he would do after fights—even after his last lover, Neal, had left him with nothing left to puzzle over.

Why did you go on this cruise, Anderson had wanted to know, and he'd said nothing, as if he were playing yet another game with Anderson and with himself. But perhaps he should have answered, he thought, looking at the water. His ironic line came back to him—"to die among the people I could never live with." How absurd a thought, how pathetically adolescent it sounded now. He always knew he wasn't going to do anything along those lines, so why pretend he might? Why did he try to fool himself that way? Who exactly was he trying to impress? Himself?

Anderson, on some level? He finished the drink he'd been carrying, felt the high, and then thought of Santa Claus Anderson and the improbable way he'd told him off. At any moment Anderson could have punched him out and perhaps killed him by sitting on him, but he stuck it to him anyway, and the thought of that made him laugh so hard it drowned out the ocean and was all he could hear in his ears for a while. Everything was making him laugh now, including the fact that he was laughing so hard. Finally he turned away from the water and began walking back to his room, thinking of Anderson's face when he told him he was gay. He was still laughing at the image of it. The old narcissist had kept him laughing a long time now. You couldn't really off yourself after meeting someone like Anderson, he thought, as he nearly bumped into a waiter. "So sorry," he said, bowing a little, "so sorry." Anderson made you too angry and then he made you laugh too hard.

Rider continued laughing down the hallway, passing people and not even covering his mouth until he reached his room and sat down on his bed. Well, he thought, after he finally calmed down, I am a twit but I've lived through my death. God, or whatever, is keeping me alive for some reason. I've lived through my death and no one could really say I'm old yet, not *old* old . . . and tomorrow we'll be in Jamaica, won't we?

DATES IN HELL

When I was a child I carried a park inside me. It must have been in my mind but it felt like it was in my body. There were different parts to the park and at a given moment I might visit any one of them. One part was a field where it was usually autumn. There were gold and red leaves blowing over the grass. In one section of the field, which was like farmland, there were cornstalks growing. In another part there was a lake—blue and still and oval, like a mirror. There were no people in or around the lake or in the woods behind it, where there was always clear light visible between the trees. There were no other people in any part of my park, ever. There was some seasonal variety—it went from spring to summer at the lake and then back to spring, whereas the field and woods rotated back and forth between early and late fall. The seasonal rotations of the world outside had little influence on my park. It followed its own laws and generated its own wind and lived inside me—the only real possession of my youth. I never discussed it with anyone, wanting to leave it unanalyzed and pure, like a secret. Otherwise people would contaminate it, I was sure.

For years my park stayed inside me and then one morning, when the sky was a whitish blue, it was gone, as if it had swum away through the milky sky while I was sleeping. After it left I felt substantially lighter, like I'd suddenly lost a great deal of weight. It was this feeling of sudden lightness that woke me up and led me to realize that my park was missing. I'd just let a boy (chronologically, a young man) have sex with me—something I was letting happen whenever they were bold enough to "force me" to. I opened my eyes, saw him next to me, smelt his awful smell (he hadn't even washed!), and realized my park was lost. Then I screamed as loud as I could and started punching him. He was too startled to fight back or talk to me—too startled to do anything but run from me—which was what I wanted.

When you lose a paradise it's not as if others are lined up to take its place. Maybe my park wasn't a paradise, but it was my only retreat. I knew retreats can't really be replaced either, or a part of me knew, but I tried anyway. I began to blindly follow my trying instincts until I saw that it wouldn't ever work.

Then I became angry at boys and stopped having sex with them. Occasionally I made love with a girl or two but found no relief there either. Instead, I passed ghostlike through the world talking only to my parents or to my teachers when they talked to me. When the pain was too intense I drank or took different drugs. Three years passed like that, maybe four. I was a young woman but I didn't feel like anything. I had thoughts I couldn't talk about, not even with myself, because there were no words to fit them. Without wanting to, I became a full-time observer of the world. I saw the mad scramble people made to have an impact but knew that even if one became the most famous person or if one had the greatest love it would all last a pitifully short time, and one would lose everything in the end. There was a built-in futility to life that was so strong it made living seem like a dream. Almost every day I felt the world was unreal, but I had to act as if it was real just in case it turned out that it really was. I felt this acting as a constant pressure, an immense burden. Why don't people just admit that they feel the same way I do? Why don't we all convene in group meetings around the world and proclaim our protest? But I never said this to anyone. Instead I continued acting.

Meanwhile my parents got divorced. My mother was even more pathetic without my father than she'd been with him. When she began to have a few lovers she became still more ridiculous, though I acted glad for her and used it all as an excuse to keep away from her and the house. Although I'd lost my park, and my thoughts continued to torment me, I still found being alone the least stressful of all possible conditions and used whatever I could to create more time with myself. For instance, my periods. Mine had always seemed so light and inconsequential I barely realized they were happening. Sometimes I wouldn't even remember to pad myself up until blood began sliding down my legs. But I heard what other women said about them and invariably used the "pain" of my periods as an excuse to lie down in my room and close the door.

There were two things I tried to do in the next group of years I faced. First I attempted to be a writer. I thought that if I described what I was observing and mixed it with some of what I was feeling it could create a kind of park inside me, clear and orderly and full of light. Instead, it was like a pointless woods, dark and densely tangled, where trees grew at contradictory angles so close to each other that one could neither walk there nor see anything.

I didn't take failure well. Personal failure alone, at that point, could make me cry, though I pretended it was my period or a cold. In spite of everything, about half the time I still thought I was intelligent and was obligated to use my mind in a way that would contribute to society—although, of course, I also loathed society. It shows how unclearly I was "thinking" that the next thing I tried to be was a therapist. I don't even want to discuss what that was like. Suffice to say the attempt stole two more years of time from my life. In my middle twenties by then, I wasn't unlike those semicubist women Picasso loved to paint with all sides of me pulsing with will and anger mixed up together and burning like fires barely under control.

Finally, I did something, in fact, several things. First, I left home and took an apartment by myself in Philadelphia. Then I got an accounting degree and eventually used it to help land a job in a small computer company that made use of my skill with numbers as well as my ability to manage people. It turned out that when I dealt with people in professional situations I was very assertive, almost as if I was the opposite of myself.

It was around then I began doing men again and in a little while started transferring my aggression at work into the whole seduction process. Instead of concentrating so much on my appearance, endlessly combing my hair and staring at myself in different clothes in the mirror, only to act like a piece of scenery at a club, I started approaching men myself and talking directly to them about what I wanted. It was surprisingly easy. I began by trying to think like a man, then to talk like a man, and finally to act like one. I found that this way I could forget the things I wanted to forget and concentrate on the present as if it were my own kind of action-painting.

Soon I was doing four or five different men a week. I had never had a real appetite before—not for sex or food or anything like that —so I had no interest in stopping it now that one had surfaced. There were nights when I had three different men, not at once (I was too scared for that), but one after the other. These were men I'd met at different late-night places. I was drinking and drugging a bit too—whatever would enhance the sensations. I still don't know how I was able to do my job at the company.

It was about this time that I slid into Hell or that Hell slid into me. I remember one night walking into a sex store looking at the toys and paraphernalia and walking out with my first strap-on. I went into the Monkey Bar a couple blocks away and sidled up to the first man I saw who was alone. He had red hair like me, though slightly blonder. He had hazel-green eyes like me, too, and looked fairly clean-cut. Strengthwise he had the advantage, weighing thirty to fifty pounds more, but I felt I could overpower him by my voice and will alone, and with the person I would soon become in bed.

It didn't take much to get him to take me back to my place. It never did.

"I got a feeling about you," I said while sitting next to him at the bar.

"What kind of feeling?" he said. I think he actually giggled a little, which normally would have been off-putting but somehow excited me, made me realize how young he was.

"That you're going to like me," I said, spreading my legs a little. I was wearing tight parachute pants with a tiny hole in the crotch and I worked my legs so my black leather boots locked around his feet. "My name's Greta."

"You're really something," he said.

"I'm glad you think so but first I want you to buy me a drink."

"I'll buy you two drinks," he said, giggling a little again. This is so easy, I thought. So fast and so easy. I'd already discovered that the less time you spent talking to a man before, the more exciting and vivid the sex would be later.

The two drinks turned into three. We lurched and laughed the whole way back to my place. Once we got inside (we didn't quite beat the rain), I threw him a towel and put a joint in his mouth as fast as I could. I already knew what I wanted to do. I got high, but I got him very high. I wanted him to be dizzy and emotional. I told him to lie on his stomach and began to lick his body. I could tell that he was even more stoned than drunk. There was a good chance my pot was laced with angel dust—it was definitely strong stuff.

"Wait there—don't move," I said once I had him spread-eagled. I slipped out of my panties and put on my strap-on in the bathroom carrying a little jar of Vaseline back with me into the room. Then I put the Vaseline all over it.

"Get your butt up in the air," I said, just sternly enough. He complied, thinking I was going to lick him some more. I reached around and grabbed his whole package with my left hand.

"What are you doing?" he mumbled—it was the last time he'd make such a modest sound.

I put my finger in him first and then my strap-on. He yelled, of course, but I didn't stop and I didn't let go of his package, either. "Just take it," I said, words that had been said to me more than once by men. All men are a little gay, I already knew, especially the womanizers, and I wasn't surprised that it worked.

"You're not a man, are you?" he said in a worried voice as soon as the pain was over.

"No, honey. This is something I bought with someone just like you in mind. This is something I bought just for you."

He was delicious, that little piece of giggling fruit, but by the next afternoon I'd forgotten him. That night I went shopping again and came back with someone even younger and more gay.

"Want to do something really freaky?" I said. He didn't say anything. I think he couldn't believe he was with someone like me and felt he was dreaming.

"I'll do it to you first and then you can do it to me." But we never got to me. He was into being hurt and between my strap-on, belt, and leather boots, he kept me constantly busy. It seemed like I was on top of him all night in complete control and when I came (with the pot kicking in just right), it felt like I was on a flying motorcycle.

But then he disappeared for me too. It was like lying next to a shadow, and in the dark, shadows are pretty much nonexistent. I couldn't wait for him to leave, though when he did (I think I even paid for his cab), I barely noticed the difference. I felt angry and vacant and unsatisfied. Immediately I wanted a man again.

It's not true that people in Hell don't realize it, just like it's not true that Hell is a place reserved for the dead. After the gay boy left I began to understand that something very basic had shifted. That the entire atmosphere of my apartment had altered, as if something had invaded it just as something had invaded my being. In the morning the feeling was just as strong, and when I went to work I took it with me. I absolutely knew I was in Hell then but had no idea what to do about it. I was like a robot with the awareness that I'd once been human but I had no idea how to get back. No options, just endless appetite. It was not the kind of thing you could tell a therapist. They were just high-class dealers anyway. Just more expensive drug dealers, in the final analysis, than the ones on the street. Besides, no matter what drug I took—and no matter what sex I did—I was still in Hell.

Though I was constantly fleeing from the past, I had very little concept of the future. The only real thing I sometimes thought about in my future was the Horror Convention. For the last two years I'd been attending the National Horror Conference in St. Louis. Years ago it was a place where people met to hear papers and have discussions about horror movies and novels, but it had evolved into a giant encounter group where people testified instead about their drug and sex addictions, their gambling and impotence and compulsive lying. The horror movies were now only shown at night, like a kind of background music. I could already picture my testimony at next year's convention (beginning the first Friday after Halloween). It gave me something to shoot for. Those people alone might understand—unless, of course, I would die for one reason or another before I made it there. It sometimes occurred to me that one of my nightly partners might murder me; that just as I turned out to be much stronger and more dominant than my skinny, small-breasted body might suggest, one of them might be more ferocious and uncontrollable as well.

It was as if fear and desire were playing a game of seesaw in the otherwise empty space inside me. When fear sent desire up in the air away from me I did nothing. I was paralyzed, knowing I was in Hell, and could only expect the worst, such as an encounter with the devil or one of his agents. Often I thought that I was the latter anyway, which would explain why Hell set up camp inside me. Then desire would assert itself as the heavier weight and chief occupant in my mind, sending fear into space, and I would go man-shopping again, in spite of the consequences, which from the law of averages alone I was convinced would ultimately lead to my sorry end.

. . . .

A strange thing was happening to my memory, too. Instead of remembering and brooding about specific people and events, as I often did when I was alone, I'd feel the essence or "feeling" of them. It was as if the museum of my past, which before had always been filled with more or less realistic works of art, was now filled only with abstract paintings. Before, I would do someone whenever thinking about another person or experience became too painful. Now I needed to do someone whenever I felt that "abstract" feeling, which often took the form of extreme heat inside me.

Still, there were no fires in Hell that I could see. I checked the thermostat ten to fifteen times a day but it stayed constant. I took my own temperature as well, which recorded a slight, ongoing fever—the only evidence, albeit ambiguous, that Hell had invaded me. After all, nothing in my apartment had been stolen or moved. I saw no apparitions or shapes (except sometimes in my slightly feverish dreams), yet everything in the apartment looked different, as if the lighting were now altered and things were either somewhat murky, as they are underwater, or preternaturally sharp.

This is the way Hell looks, I remember thinking, but what good does knowledge do if your life remains the same? Every day I was the same barely functioning zombie at work, desperately trying to hide my secret.

Every night I was still the man predator with my strap-on and other sex tools, which I was spending all my extra money on.

Then one night, with my hair slicked back and tied up and wearing my strap-on under my parachute pants, I went to a girl's bar instead. It required talking to one for a while, which I actually enjoyed, and even that I do a couple of dances, pressing the girl I picked up against my strap-on during the slow numbers. I left with her a couple of hours after that. I remembered her name, Thea (a rarity for me as far as my partners were concerned), because it was unusual and I liked it. In my mind I gave her the nickname Definite article / Indefinite article—which was something that seemed descriptive of me, too. It had been years since I'd been with a woman and I was simultaneously relieved and disappointed to discover that sexually it didn't make much of a difference. A few minor technical adjustments were all. I remember telling her that I was almost always with men and she didn't believe me, which I took as a compliment. I thought it didn't matter whether I was with men or women. I thought nothing mattered except the fire inside me and putting out the fire and then feeling it again, which was the rhythm of Hell. But that night, sleeping next to Thea (which in itself was unusual since I invariably sent my partners home after doing them), I had a powerful dream. In the first part of the dream I was trying to figure out if I was a man or a woman. I was shouting the question into the lake in my old park, which reflected me like a mirror, waiting for it to answer me. But if the answer did come, it was ambiguous. Finally a clear response came from the lake in the form of an image. I saw a picture of a big-toothed white shark and realized that's what I really was—a shark in a feeding frenzy that felt alive only when eating. But the sensation of eating never lasted long, so the shark always needed food.

When I woke up I was unusually upset, even by Hell's standards. The worst part of it was I couldn't even be sure my dream wasn't a trick of Hell, that even my dreams weren't Hell-tainted. Thea was still sleeping so I walked into my kitchen and drank the remains of an emergency bottle of vodka. When I came back to the room tears were streaming down my face and I was shaking a lot. The next thing I must have done was to wake up Thea, who held me in her arms without saying much, just little comforting things until my shaking was more or less under control. That's when I told her a little about being in Hell, that I wasn't speaking in metaphors but meant an actual, palpable, physical place, though it had also taken up residence inside me so that I brought a part of it to work with me in the daytime and to the bars with me at night.

She didn't say much to that. She was trying to show support, which I appreciated. I was surprised that I was trying so hard to convince her. "It's a myth that Hell is a place bad people are sent to after they die. Hell travels to people, it's portable and it completely controls your environment. It sets up residence inside and outside you."

"So I guess I'm in Hell too," Thea said with a kind of sad smile. She had hazel eyes like me but hers were hazel blue.

"I wouldn't blame you a bit for leaving," I said.

"I don't want to leave but I would like you to go out for lunch with me. My treat. There's a new Chinese restaurant with a great buffet, or we could go to a Cuban place."

I looked at her in the hard way I have of looking at people. The Hell atmosphere was still in the room but a little white light (like the light in the spaces between the trees in my old park) had broken through and danced around her. I was afraid to comment on it but noticed that it hadn't completely left.

"So what do you think?"

"Anything is possible," I said, touching her hair, "isn't it?"

The dancing light had disappeared but I still liked looking at her eyes, which were oval and quite blue in the morning light. The lake, I thought, as I put on my clothes. The lake is back.

We walked hand in hand to the Chinese restaurant. Thea didn't seem surprised that she wasn't in Hell. I felt cautiously optimistic that it might slowly lift from me too but didn't want to act too grateful or astonished. I clung close to her, however. She did almost all the talking on our walk there as well as during the meal. She was talking about how everything in the universe was meant to cancel everything else out in an almost mathematical way to attain equilibrium. The amount of fear in the world was matched by and in some way inextricable from the amount of desire. Good and evil, success and failure, light and dark, and life and death were similarly balanced. To move away from this principle—even to believe you could—was to experience chaos or Hell.

She was still talking about this when we left the restaurant. I had been holding hands with her for the whole meal but to revive my circulation I let go for a second. Immediately a mist blown in by a sudden wind enveloped her. I didn't hear her scream. I didn't hear myself scream either and to this day don't know if I did or not. (I'll talk about this in an hour to my group at the conference.) In a matter of seconds this light-colored but impenetrable mist had covered her and carried her off. (It looked almost like steam rising from a giant air vent.) It all lasted only a few seconds and no one else in the vicinity saw it or acted concerned. I would definitely have screamed and been shaken to my core, but I immediately discovered that, along with Thea, the mist had taken Hell away from me too.

DUCK PILLS

I didn't want to make the King nervous but I couldn't help getting closer to the rail. We were up so high and outside the glass walls of The Link, the city was shining with all its Christmas lights. Then the glass walls ended.

"Give me your hand," he said. "Let's walk in the middle of the floor."

"Why, Daddy? I'm not going to fall over."

"Just indulge me," the King said. "Just do it for me."

We were on The Link, which connected the hotel with all the stores and restaurants and movie theaters, and maybe the rest of Kansas City, too. The King said The Link was bigger than Kansas City, which made me laugh.

Then the glass wall returned and we walked closer to the rail, but I kept my hand in his anyway. I saw birds lit up in gold, the giant Christmas tree outside with the star on top, and lights draped over the tree like a long necklace it was wearing.

We got lost on The Link. When we finally were back in the room I made my pillow tower and my pillow slide and, with a little help from the King, my sheet tent. I was back in my bed and he was bending over me.

"Didn't we have a special day today?"

"Yah. We got lost on The Link three times," I said laughing, "every time we went out to eat."

The King laughed and said, "That's true, but besides that didn't we have some special moments today?"

"Yes Daddy."

"It's important to have special moments. My father wanted to have them with me. He wanted to take me on trips so we could have special moments too, but he was always busy with his work. I'll never be too busy to take trips with you, though, never. Even now that you'll be with mom most of the time. Do you understand?"

"Yes Daddy."

Then the King closed the book he'd been reading to me and kissed my hair like he always did.

. . . .

We were in Loose Park looking for the duck pond. I'd been making maps in the hotel when the King said we had to go outside.

"Why? Why do we have to go outside?"

"We didn't travel six hours just to stay in a hotel room, that's why," he said.

The King made a deal with me—saying I could pick any place on the map of Kansas City and we'd go there. I picked Loose Park because the name was so funny, as if it had just escaped from its leash.

"Do you think Loose Park will still be there when we get there or do you think it will have run away?" the King said to me in the cab and I laughed.

I didn't have to wear a coat. It was fifty-two degrees, but the pond was still half frozen anyway. We brought some bread from a bakery in The Link, but the ducks ignored our food. It was as if they were under a spell or maybe just very stupid ducks, like the King said.

We walked on and on through Loose Park. It was very wide and scattered.

"This park needs a link," the King said, and we both laughed again. Finally we came to a children's playground and I played there the rest of the afternoon.

. . . .

We got lost on The Link again that night. My legs hurt from walking, and I went to my bed quickly.

"Daddy, when are we going home?"

The King had just finished reading me a story. Every night I had "creative time" during which I drew maps before he'd read to me. I used to write stories during creative time about the animal characters the King and I made up, like Baby Claw, Tail, Happy Hedgehog, Tiny Duck, and Duckling Van Duckling, but now I just drew maps of cities like Chicago or Kansas City, or of Clawton and Hogtown. On the maps I drew and labeled the important streets, avenues, and highway signs.

"Do you miss home?" the King said, eying me carefully.

"I don't know."

"I thought we'd take one more trip since it's our vacation and there are so many things to see. Don't you want to see more things?"

"I don't know."

"I thought we'd go to New Orleans for a few days. It's a big beautiful city in Louisiana."

"Of course it's in Louisiana. But it's not the capital. Baton Rouge is."

"You're right. You know all the capitals of all the states, don't you?"

"Yes Daddy."

"I bet you're the only kid in third grade who knows them all . . . You have an amazing memory. It's a gift. We shouldn't be ashamed or embarrassed about our gifts. Most of life is a search for our gifts, so when we know we have one it should make us happy."

The King stopped and looked right at my eyes. I looked back into his but didn't say anything.

"You are my gift," said the King. "I used to be a painter but now you are my work of art. Do you think you'll have children one day too?"

"I don't know."

"What do you mean, you don't know? Don't you want to have kids?"

"Yes."

"Then why wouldn't you?"

"I just don't think I'm the kind of kid who will."

"That's ridiculous. If you want to have children you will," the King said, but he looked sad after he said that. Then he kissed my hair.

. . . .

The next day we left The Link. We were moving again—this time to New Orleans. We never stayed in any place too long. The King was packing both our suitcases while I lay on top of the bed watching him. I knew he wanted me to help but I was mad and didn't want to. Every few minutes he poured from a bottle on the desk into a glass. It was alcohol, I knew, 'cause I could smell it.

"Why are we moving, Daddy?"

"We're not moving, because we don't live here. We were just visiting Kansas City."

"You mean The Link," I said, correcting him.

"The Link, and now we're visiting New Orleans."

"But I don't want to. I don't want to leave The Link."

"We have to, it's not always a question of what you want."

"But why do we have to?"

"I have some work to do there," he said, finishing another glass.

"I thought you said we were going there for fun?"

"It can be both," the King said.

"Do you have to make a painting?"

"I have to sell some paintings. I explained this to you before, didn't I?"

"I don't know."

"When I was young I used to make paintings. A long time ago, right? When you are young you make things and when you are old you sell them. You still don't understand that. Everything in our society is determined by the need for money. You don't know that yet, but you will."

We were quiet while I thought about what he said. At least he'd stopped packing now and was looking at me, though far away from me at the same time.

"What do you think is the most important thing?" the King said. He often asked me questions like that.

"Playing," I said, with a smile.

He laughed a little. "That's a good answer. In a way you're right, actually."

"Playing doesn't have anything to do with making money."

"It shouldn't but it does."

"What do you mean?"

"Toys cost money to buy, don't they? And the ads on TV that make you want to buy them cost a *lot* of money. Toys and entertainment are probably the biggest business in the world, bigger even than food. It's to the point where all of us view the world as if it exists to entertain us. That's the tragedy of it. We listen to people discussing the war on TV and we think 'that's interesting,' forgetting that real people are killing each other there—over money, of course."

We looked at each other. I wanted to change the subject. "Daddy, did you ever paint maps when you used to make paintings?"

"No, I didn't."

"Did you ever draw them?"

"No. That's your area of expertise. Why don't you draw a map now while I finish packing?"

"I'm not going to draw a map. I'm going to draw a clock instead. It's going to show how many hours we have left in The Link."

. . . .

We were in another hotel, in New Orleans, and the King was about to tell me something—probably that we had to go outside. I was drawing a clock tower, but mostly I was drawing a clock.

"I've decided something important," he said. I kept my face down over my sketch pad on the bed. "Don't you want to know what it is?"

"What Daddy?"

"I've decided to be completely honest with you—that is, if you'll be completely honest with me."

I kept my head down and continued drawing.

"Will you?"

"What?" I said, looking up, pen in hand.

"Will you be completely honest and never lie to me?"

"Yes Daddy."

"In the end it's all we've got, our honesty, don't you think?"

I didn't answer and continued drawing. It was 7:11 (my favorite time) on the clock I was drawing but it was 7:29 on the bedroom clock.

"I'm going to have to start to do things a little differently now that I'm not with mom anymore."

"What do you mean?"

"I'm going to have to sometimes do things for myself, even though you may not like it."

"Why Daddy?"

"Because I need to. Because I need to take care of myself as well as you or I'll become unhappy and then I won't do a good job of taking care of you. Can you stop drawing for a minute and look at me?"

I put down my pen and looked at the King.

"It's important that you understand I love you just as much even when I'm doing things I need to do instead of the thing you want me to do for you. Do you understand that?"

"I don't know."

"I think you do and I think you will. Tonight, for example, I have to meet a man and I could be meeting some other people too and you're going to have to go with me."

"But I don't want to go out. I just want to draw."

"But you know I can't leave you here."

"Yes you can. I don't want to meet any people."

"I know you don't like to meet people but this is one of those times I told you about when I need to do something. This is about work and making money, OK?"

"I don't know."

"But I know. You have to do it. I don't want to fight with you, Jimmy. I just want you to leave with me in about thirty minutes and I'm going to have to comb your hair. You've got a worse bed-head than Happy Hedgehog."

. . . .

We were walking up a long flight of stairs. It was like walking up a frozen waterfall that went on forever. When we finally got to the top we were in the man's apartment. He had a beard that he kept touching. His name was Gus.

"Gus, this is my son, Jimmy."

"Hey Jimmy," Gus said, sticking out his hand.

"Say hello, Jimmy," the King said. I looked down at the floor. "He's very shy," the King said.

"That's OK," Gus said, mussing my hair. I didn't like that he touched my hair. I wanted to bite him.

The apartment had at least four rooms, long hallways with lots of turns, and a balcony. There were paintings all over the walls. I thought about drawing a map of it but instead I ran around and around while the King talked to Gus.

When I finally stopped I walked into the living room, where the King and Gus were sitting on a sofa, and watched them. There were paintings on the wall above them and a fire in the fireplace.

"I think we've covered all the bases," the King said, looking at Gus. "I know you can handle it."

"I can handle it. You saw. I can do de Chiricos in my sleep."

"You do better work than I did. That's why I got into another part of the business."

"Thank you."

"You know, they say very good things about you in New York."

"Thank you again."

"Anyway, I'll be coming back to look, say in . . . well, you tell me when."

"I can do it in a week if I have to. How soon do you really need it?"

"We've got some time. We're not in a big rush. We just moved something a couple months ago."

"Give me two more weeks then and you'll get a masterpiece, a fucking foolproof masterpiece."

"Hey," the King said to Gus, gesturing toward me with his head.

"Oh, sorry," Gus said, covering his mouth with his hand for a moment. "Does he know what it means?"

"I don't know. I don't know what he knows."

"Well, I'm sorry . . . I'll watch my language. Listen, can you stay and meet Nadine? She'll be here in a few minutes. I think you'll like her."

"That would be difficult."

"Come on, have a little fun. Have you eaten yet?"

"Kind of. Jimmy eats early."

"Well at least have a drink and meet Nadine. You deserve a reward. I'm buying, OK? My way of saying thank you. Come on, you're the King—you deserve it."

I stared at Gus and felt my heart thump. How did he know what I called him? How could he say it when I never did?

"I'll have to talk to the little guy."

The King walked toward me and I looked down at the floor again.

"It won't be much longer, OK?"

"I want to go to the hotel."

"I know you do, buddy, but it really won't be much longer. We're going to take a walk, a nice woman's going to come over, and we're going to take a walk and then we'll go to the hotel."

"No, I want to go back to the hotel now."

"Remember what we talked about?"

"What?"

"About honesty and me having to do certain things."

I didn't say anything.

"Look, if you do this and are nice I'll buy you any toy you want tomorrow."

"*Any* toy?"

"That's right. We'll find a toy store tomorrow—we'll make that our first order of business—and you can pick out anything you want. Is that a deal?"

I thought about it. I thought about buying a book of maps or a clock. "Yes Daddy," I said, "it's a deal."

. . . .

It was dark in the restaurant, too dark to run around. There was smoke in the restaurant that tickled my nose and it was loud like a zoo. I sat next to the King and held his hand. I wanted to draw a map of the way to mom's house from New Orleans—just the main routes and highways and their speed limits, but it was too dark to draw, at least to draw something as complicated as a map. Instead I started thinking about drawing a clock to show the King how late it was. Then I thought of something. What if the hands fell off a clock? What if in the restaurant the hands fell off all the clocks and watches? Then there would be no other way to know how late it was except by looking at my drawing. My drawing would be a very important thing then. But how could I do it? This wasn't one of those restaurants where they gave you crayons and a coloring book. All I had was a napkin and a spoon.

Gus suddenly got up from the table. He said goodbye to me and tried to touch my hair but I shrank away from him so he couldn't reach me. I thought we'd be going home then but the King continued drinking and talking to Nadine. She laughed a lot, like a clown on TV. I felt nervous in my stomach remembering when the King drank at mom's house how he'd usually yell. She'd yell at him too and say things about his women until the yelling was louder than a zoo, even louder than an ambulance.

"Daddy, I wanna go back to the hotel," I suddenly said.

The King didn't say anything but gave my hand a squeeze. He was turned toward Nadine, who was wearing a short skirt with her sweater unbuttoned even though it was winter, just like a clown. She had very white teeth and red painted lips. I looked away from her and thought about the handless clock. When I turned to look again the King was kissing her.

"Daddy, I want to go home now," I said, freeing my hand from his. He turned toward me with a scared look on his face.

"OK, Champ, we'll get going now. Nadine's gonna walk with us back to the hotel. You can do that, right?" he said to her.

"Sure, if you want."

Then he whispered something in her ear before he finally got up from the table. I stood up and grabbed his left hand. He was taking too long to leave the restaurant, talking and laughing with Nadine. I'd never seen a woman laugh as much as her. I'd never seen a kid laugh that much either—not even the silliest kid in my class.

"Come on. Why is it taking so long?" I said. When we finally got outside on the sidewalk she tried to talk to me but I turned my head away from her. I was walking on the outside nearest the street (something that the King usually wouldn't allow because it made him nervous). The King was in the middle and Nadine was closest to the buildings. I was seeing the hotel room in my mind. Maybe when we got back we could still play one of our pillow games if it wasn't too late. I tried picturing a clock to try to guess what time it was but I couldn't quite see it.

"It won't be long, Champ," the King said to me, as if he were reading my mind—something he was usually very good at, just like he was a magician and it was a trick he knew. Then he turned toward Nadine and started talking and laughing with her again, which, of course, only made the walk take longer. I decided to listen to them for a while—having nothing else to do.

"So were you a painter once too?" the King asked her.

"Me? No never, I never was."

"Really? Seems like everyone in our group was a painter once. Well, that's refreshing."

"I did do some modeling for painters for a while."

"Here in New Orleans?"

"Yuh . . . at the university, and privately."

"I can see why. Your body is quite the work of art."

"Thank youuu," she said, saying the *u* for a long time and laughing again. It was like laughing was the thing she did best in the world so she did it all the time.

We crossed the street. There was a lot of noise and light up ahead. The noise was mostly music and the light was blinding, like looking at the sun.

"That's Bourbon Street," Nadine said. "Wanna check it out?"

"I would but I promised Jimmy we'd go straight back to the hotel. I think I'll do that on my next visit with you if you'd like."

"It's mostly a tourist trap anyway, but sometimes it's fun if you're in that type of mood . . . Hey, what're you thinking about? You seem kind of far away."

"I was thinking about you doing that private modeling actually . . . in the painters' studios."

"I shouldn't have told you that."

"No, not at all, I admire that. It's like the last link to a lost world of . . . personal service."

"What do you mean?"

"I mean there used to be a milkman who delivered your milk, there used to be a doctor who came to your house, there used to be an operator who handled your calls, there used to be a gas attendant who said 'How're you doing?' Now they've all disappeared. The money's still there, but the people have disappeared. It's like people used to work for money but now money works against people. What you used to do contradicts that pattern, so I admire it."

"Wow, I'd never thought of it like that. You've got a really deep mind. You sure you wanna see me again? I'm not exactly the world's brightest."

"I'm absolutely sure. I'd love to. But meanwhile we're still going to stick to our plan, aren't we?"

"Sure, if you still want to."

"The buffet in the hotel is pretty good. Here, take my credit card and charge it to my room. Just have them call me if there's any problem or call me on my cell and I'll speak to them."

"I don't think I'll be eating anything."

"Why not?"

"A girl's gotta keep her figure."

"Well, have a drink then, and in half an hour or forty-five minutes we'll, you know, continue . . ."

"Yuh, I know," she said.

We were outside the Fairmount Hotel now, where we were staying.

"Bye-bye Jimmy," Nadine said, getting down almost on her knees and trying to look at my eyes.

"Say goodbye," the King said, but I kept my head down, then walked through the revolving doors into the hotel.

When we got back to the room I decided to forgive the King. I felt happy and jumped up and down on the bed while we told a story about Tail and Baby Claw building an amusement park in Clawtown. The King asked me if I wanted him to read to me or if we should tell a story and I picked telling a story like we used to. Sometimes I'd get down from the bed and run around the room while we told it.

Meanwhile the King kept looking at his watch and I worried about bedtime coming soon, so I made a lot of funny and outrageous things happen in the story, bringing in Happy Hedgehog and Duckling Van Duckling (the world's smartest animal) to help trick Mrs. Fullclaw, Baby Claw's mean teacher, into coming to the amusement park so Baby Claw could get his revenge on her for all the times she'd mistreated him. But then Baby Claw took a duck pill by accident. They were pills that Duck invented that made you stupid, because Duck was the stupidest animal in the world. Soon Baby Claw started doing silly and crazy things. I was laughing and jumping on the bed and the King was laughing too. Then he looked at his watch again and said, "Hey, buddy, it's time to calm down and get under the covers. It's past your bedtime."

"No it isn't. How can you say that?"

"Yes, it very nearly is."

"It's not my bedtime for fifteen minutes."

"All right, but you need to do something . . . calmer. You need to have creative time now."

"But creative time is always for at least an hour."

"You need to have a shortened version of creative time. Why don't you draw something? Why don't you draw a clock?"

The King put my paper and pen in front of me and for a while I thought I'd draw a magic clock that would say 8 instead of 9, that would never go past 8 so I wouldn't have to go to bed. But I began drawing a map instead.

The King stopped watching me, still thinking I was drawing a clock probably, and went into the bathroom. I heard the shower go on. It sounded loud in my ears, like a waterfall. Later I heard him brushing his teeth at the sink. When he came back to the bed he smelled different, like gum or peaches.

"It's bedtime now, honey," he said. "What did you draw?"

"A map."

"Can I see it?"

I moved away from the map I was hovering over.

"Very good. What's it a map of?"

"It's a map of the way back to mom's house from here. Just the major roads and highways."

"Oh," said the King. He had a strange look on his face. Then he told me he loved me and shut my light off and, saying good night, bent down and kissed my hair.

I had a feeling I'd have trouble getting to sleep but I lay still and kept my eyes closed anyway, as if I really was sleeping. The King wasn't sleeping either. There was a hall light on that was half blocked by a wall, but all the other lights were off. I could hear the King moving back and forth through the room and then in and out of the bathroom, as if he was packing or getting ready for something. I wanted to ask him what he was doing but couldn't since I was supposed to be asleep. Then he came up to my bed and whispered my name to be sure I was sleeping and I stayed completely quiet.

When the knocking came I almost said something but didn't. I was surprised at how still I was being, surprised too that my eyes stayed closed though my ears were open.

I heard voices in the hallway and opened my ears even more.

"Is it OK?"

"Wait a second," then the King walked up to my bed to check on me again. "He's sound asleep. Come on in."

"Are you sure?"

"Believe me, it takes a lot to wake him."

It was Nadine's voice and I wondered what she was doing here when she'd already said goodbye. The voices stayed in the hallway.

"How was the buffet?" the King said.

"I didn't have any. I told you I wasn't going to have any."

"So you were a good girl?"

"Not completely."

"Really? Tell Daddy what happened?"

"I had a couple of drinks. I was going to bring you one but I was extra bad and had it on the way up."

"You were bad, but no problem, I just happen to have a refrigerator stocked full of liquid entertainment."

She laughed again.

"Liquid entertainment—I like that. That would be a good title for an album."

"Not to mention a porn movie."

Nadine laughed again.

"So come on in. He's asleep."

"Should I?"

"Absolutely."

"Your little boy doesn't seem to like me very much."

"He's just shy."

"Really?"

"Yuh, really. He has a mild form of autism actually. It's called Asperger's syndrome."

"I'm sorry."

"Don't be. He's a happy kid most of the time and amazingly smart in certain ways. It's just hard for him to interact with people—kids even more than adults. Come on, let's open that refrigerator, OK?"

I heard their footsteps, heard the King open the refrigerator, and I wondered what the "asparagus" thing meant. When I got my concentration back Nadine was talking.

"I know about kids too. I had, have a kid, too, you know."

"I didn't know."

"Reason I said 'had' is she lives with her father now. He won custody 'cause of the trouble I was in, you know, the legal stuff I told you about."

"I'm sorry."

"I mean with drugs, I didn't have a chance, right? So I lost her a couple years ago. I'm only allowed a few days to see her—well a little more than that—but the visits have to be supervised. The funny thing is I only did the drugs to please the man I was with but the man didn't really care and when I realized it, it was too late. It's just like he tore out my heart when he took her. It's like he ruined me, you know?"

"Jesus, that's awful. I'm really sorry. If I lost Jimmy like that I'd go crazy . . . You know there was a time I used to be so nervous about him getting, say, hit by a car or something that I didn't even want him to leave the house. I blame myself for that."

"Yah, I hear you. I know what worry is. I worry all the time. I sure hope I don't ever get in trouble again for anything."

"Don't worry about that with us. Like Gus says, 'It's fucking foolproof.' Your part especially."

"Yah."

"Yah."

They both laughed then and I heard their glasses clink. Then their voices turned to whispers and stopped and came back on and stopped again, like someone kept pressing the mute button back and forth on a TV remote. I head kissing sounds next. Then Nadine said, "I brought you something else, too."

I think I fell asleep then, but just for seventeen minutes. It was about 10:45 when I fell asleep and 11:02 when I woke up. The first thing I noticed after waking up was the smoke that smelled different from any smoke I'd ever smelled before.

"Daddy," I said. "Daddy." I could tell right away he wasn't in the room. I jumped out of bed and followed the light and smoke to the bathroom, where the door was closed. I could hear the waterfall sound of the bathtub running and when I leaned against the door I could hear them laughing and talking. Then the water roar stopped and I could hear them better.

"I can see why you're a model."

"That was a long time ago."

"Believe me, you still got it. Oh yes . . . just like that, just like that, don't stop."

I knocked on the door, not as hard as I could, but pretty hard. "Daddy, I've got to pee."

"Shit," the King muttered.

"Daddy I've got to pee," I said louder.

"Do it in your pull-ups, OK?"

"No, Daddy, I have to use the bathroom."

"Wait a second."

I could hear him getting out of the tub and unlocking the door.

"OK, it's open," he said.

When I opened the door I saw his naked body with bubble-bath soap decorating his wet skin as he opened the shower curtain to get back in the tub. Then he pulled the curtain shut. There was no more talking or laughing now. I could see part of Nadine through a little opening in the curtain when I turned my head. Then I peed.

"Shut the door and go back to sleep," the King said angrily. I felt like I was going to cry but didn't. I went out of the bathroom but I didn't shut the door completely.

"I should go," Nadine said.

"You don't have to."

"No, I do. I never meant to cause trouble with you and your little boy. I mean . . ."

"You didn't cause trouble. This is no big deal."

"No, it's not right. I never learn my lesson not to mix business with pleasure. I never learn."

"I'm sorry this happened. I . . ."

"No. I'm sorry. It was a nice beginning though. You still want me for the job, right? You and Gus still want me."

"Of course, of course. Nothing's changed. I'll call you tomorrow."

"Yah, you'll call. It's like calling Miss Bad Luck person to person."

"I'll call. Of course I'll call. You were good luck for me tonight, real good luck."

"OK. Can you bring me my clothes, do you think?"

"You got money for a cab?" the King said. I could hear him getting out of the bathtub and I ran back to bed and pulled the covers up.

I could hear the King walking around, then dropping something, probably a shoe, then walking back into the bathroom. I heard him talking softly to Nadine but I didn't hear the words.

I closed my eyes, not to sleep but to see the giant clock rising yellow and empty like a sun. I kind of squinted in the dark and then I could see its hands, even the second hand, and I counted because I didn't want to hear Nadine anymore. I counted 122 seconds on the clock and then I stopped when I heard the door shut.

The King was talking in the voice he used when he was talking to himself. I heard him open the refrigerator and pour something. I heard him drink it and put the glass down on the table beside our beds. Then he sat down on my bed.

"Jimmy, are you awake?"

I didn't say anything. I still wanted him to think I was asleep.

"I'm sorry. I guess I must have taken a duck pill tonight, huh? Are you asleep, really asleep? I don't blame you for being mad," he said, "you'll have to learn that I make mistakes . . . it's like getting lost on The Link. I'm just far from perfect, right? I'm just much too weak sometimes. It's not that I want to be but there are things that make us that way just like with Baby Claw and the duck pill, right?"

He reached for the glass and drank from it. I heard it fall from his hand onto the carpet. He had a different smell that scared me.

I felt myself cry but I didn't make any noise. He continued talking but I could barely hear what he was saying and it didn't sound like him anyway.

Then he lay down next to me and soon began snoring. I looked for the yellow clock with my eyes closed to help count myself to sleep but I only saw dots like lots of sun spots. So I sat up and opened my eyes and thought about trying to see a map but decided I didn't want to and decided I didn't want to see The Link either. I thought I would just count without seeing anything.

I closed my eyes. You couldn't ever tell when sleep would come. I counted "122, 121, 120 . . ." Then I lay down next to the sleeping King.

THE CONFERENCE ON
BEAUTIFUL MOMENTS

From both his reading and the interviews he'd con-
ducted with former members, Dansforth was convinced that in recent
years the conference had undergone a major change. What had begun
twenty years ago as a celebration of beautiful, transformative moments
in the arts had in essence become a celebration of beautiful, transformative moments in the members' personal lives about which they were more
than eager to testify. Like so many other institutions, the conference had
simply shifted its emphasis from the aesthetic to the confessional and in
the process seen its popularity dramatically increase. While it was true
that Dansforth would have liked to attend some of the lectures offered
in past years, like "Spiritual Issues in Mahler's 'Das Lied von der Erde' "
or "The Sense of the Apocalyptic in Kandinsky," it would have been an
impossible sell for his newspaper. Why would his alternative weekly (or
any other newspaper, for that matter) be interested in a bunch of profes-
sors or would-be artists talking about Cézanne or Satie? But to cover the
twentieth anniversary of an organization at which people expounded on
their extraterrestrial encounters, out-of-body revelations, or newfound
orgasmic powers had a far greater appeal.

So it was that Dansforth (who was always angling to do articles that
allowed him to travel) convinced his bosses to fully fund his trip and let
him write a feature on the conference, provided he keep his true purpose
hidden. The plan was for him to appear to be a full-fee-paying, first-time

member from his home city of St. Louis named Stanley Seely (they'd provided him with complete fake identification because Seely was recently deceased and there was a certain physical resemblance) the better to ultimately deliver a more candidly funny report on what his editor called "the conference of lunatics."

As he finished unpacking at the end of the first uneventful day at the conference he was surprised at the relative tawdriness of the location they'd chosen for this spring's meeting. Not that, all things considered, St. Petersburg Beach wasn't an attractive spot (although the relentless procession of hotels, stores, and restaurants along Beach Boulevard was almost vulgar), but it could hardly compare with the beauty of past conference sites in Santa Barbara, Vancouver, or Maui. Maybe it was yet another sign of the more practical orientation of the conference's new board of directors, since it was obviously a lot less expensive to go to a place like St. Petersburg and would therefore attract more people.

He was still thinking about this after breakfast the next day. "The Conference of Impeccable Finance," Dansforth said to himself cynically, as he dragged a comb through his thinning dark hair. He realized, suddenly, that he had to hurry—there was a meeting in the mid-sized hotel's ballroom—the first event of the day. Normally, Dansforth was an oblivious dresser, but realizing he had to blend in with the other members, he was now wearing a multicolored sports shirt and a pair of lemon-colored pants he'd bought the afternoon before.

The ballroom, which had a view of the beach that didn't quite include the ocean, contained a plethora of tables, at each of which six people were seated. Because he'd taken a wrong turn coming out of the elevator, he was a few minutes late and had missed the director's opening remarks and, indeed, any definitive sighting of the director, as well. A security guard indicated which table he was to report to but refused to speculate on what the topic of discussion might be. Pay attention, Dansforth told himself as he approached the table, reminding himself that to preserve his "identity" he couldn't take notes until he was back in his hotel room. The conference actively discouraged note taking as a distraction from "true listening," and he couldn't risk drawing attention to himself by defying their recommended policy.

The mostly middle-aged members at his table (three of each sex) smiled benignly enough as he introduced himself and apologized for being late. Quickly he realized that all members were expected to report on their experience of beauty in their lives, specifically in the year since last spring's conference. A man named Peter Traynor, a retired businessman and philanthropist, according to his card, was speaking in an odd manner that was both intense and strangely clipped. He had a short haircut, unusually white, tightly drawn skin, and a face on which some kind of work had been done making it impossible to tell his age.

"I did address last year's issues," Traynor was saying to a woman named Madeline, whom Dansforth soon surmised was the group leader, perhaps even a prominent member of the staff.

"With good results, I hope," Madeline said.

Traynor shrugged.

"Were you able to get over your 'tainted day' obsession?"

A brief spot of color appeared in Traynor's face. "The twenty-four-hour cycle per se is not so important to me as it was."

"I'm not sure what he's talking about," said a Chinese American woman named Joy.

"Peter used to be overly concerned with trying to have a day in which nothing painful or disappointing happened," said Madeline, with a hostess-type smile firmly in place. "I'm glad you got rid of that," she added. "I'll bet you've experienced more beauty than ever now."

Traynor paused, the strained expression on his face seemed to make his skin stretch even tighter. "Yes and no," he said.

For the first time Madeline looked somewhat nonplussed. "Can you explain?"

"I became very focused on finding a pure moment of beauty, something uncorrupted by anything unbeautiful, and I began searching for it in various parts of the world. I'd gotten reports about Vancouver, did some research and thought it seemed possible there. So I went with high hopes even though my trip to Peru the month before had been so . . . disappointing."

Dansforth wanted to ask where he got all the money to go on these beauty safaris but held his tongue.

"I'd heard that Stanley Park was the place to go to find beauty in Vancouver, so I set off on a mostly sunny day the first morning after I arrived. There was a seawall that the natives advised me to walk along, which wound in semicircles but eventually led to the park. There were extraordinary things to see on the seawall walk. The thick green forest around the water, the green islands and snow-capped mountains."

"Sounds beautiful," Madeline said, hopefully.

"It was *almost* beautiful," Traynor said, his eyes twitching two or three times. "Problem was the goddamned Olympics."

"I don't understand," Joy blurted, then quickly covered her mouth, before mumbling "sorry for interrupting."

"Vancouver is getting the Olympics in 2010 and they're already doing massive construction for it. Along the seawall you could see—you couldn't help but see—the giant cranes and trucks. They were digging up the earth and draining the water, all to make way for new stores and hotels, and they were making a racket, an inescapable racket. Between the tall boats in the harbor and the huge cranes, the view of the mountains was also almost completely blocked. Still, I felt encouraged when I left the seawall, crossed the street, and walked into the park itself. There I saw green fields, at first, that sloped uphill, but I could still see the top parts of the cranes working near the bay. I could even still hear them, a horrid kind of buzzing sound like a war going on, so I headed for the woods."

Joy put her hand over her mouth in an expression of empathy, while a different kind of expression, a mix of exasperation and concern, flashed across Madeline.

"When the buzzing got more intense, I thought I was about to be bombed and dropped down to my knees behind a rock. Looking up I saw a plane, flying not too far over my head, a repellant helicopter giving some tourists an aerial view of the park.

"When the plane left, I ran for the deeper part of the woods. More planes were flying. Was I crazy to suppose a park is supposed to be a quiet place in which to contemplate nature? Instead, it was like a war going on and I found myself running off the path to protect myself from this outrage of noise, this *rape* of the atmosphere."

"Did you escape?" Joy said, with her black eyes opened wide to a comical degree. This time Dansforth chuckled, which he quickly tried to camouflage with a few faux coughs.

"Only momentarily," Traynor said, with a pained smile. "There were puddles everywhere and beyond them a pond where the ducks swam. It was just too damn wet and cold to stay in that part of the woods. Through the trees I could see a sliver of the rose gardens. I had a decision to make: rose gardens or pond, pond or rose gardens. I went to the pond because I've always loved the majesty of ducks, dumb though they are.

"I approached the pond carefully, not wanting to disturb the ducks, which, tourist weary, couldn't have cared less if I walked an inch from their webbed feet. Still, I felt I was about to experience the very essence of beauty when it came again. The hideous roaring of the tourist war planes flying over the pond. A minute later a second plane came. That was the end of Vancouver for me . . . it was a crushing disappointment," he said, pounding his fist on the table, which caused some milk from his cereal bowl to overflow.

Dansforth noticed that Madeline, whom he was sitting next to, had pressed a green button on a box about the size of a cell phone that was resting on her lap. He wondered why he hadn't seen it before or how it had suddenly appeared.

"Peter, are you all right?" Madeline said. Traynor looked at her with an equal mix of surprise and suspicion, but said nothing. "I think you'd benefit by talking to Sidney now. I think it would do you good to spend a little time with him."

Traynor looked at her with a fierce and frightened expression, like a head in a Van Gogh painting, Dansforth thought.

"What's going on?" said Elliot, a thin middle-aged man with wire-rimmed glasses who sat across from Dansforth. As far as Dansforth knew those were the first words he'd spoken at the meeting.

'I don't need to see Sidney," Traynor said softly, but adamantly. "You sent for him, didn't you?"

"He'll help you just like he did before. We agreed to this as a condition of your attending this year, remember?"

"I let myself get too dependent on all of you," Traynor said, "and you just want my money."

"Who's Sidney?" Elliot said, and the semi-obese redhead named Kathy, who sat beside him, nodded to indicate she was wondering the same thing.

"Sidney is part of our staff. He helps people when they're upset and have lost their spiritual equilibrium. He helps them refocus in a more positive way on . . . the beautiful moments—and isn't that why we're all here? Peter will feel much better after he talks with him, he always does."

Kathy made another identical nod, but Elliot looked skeptical and Joy's froglike mouth opened again.

"I don't need to see Sidney. I don't need reorientation," Traynor said, suddenly rising from the table. "I'm going back to my room."

Traynor walked away from the table with long lurching strides toward the end of the ballroom, where an equally tall man who appeared to be considerably younger met him and soon accompanied him out of the room.

"He's upset," Madeline said. "He's suffering unnecessarily."

"Obviously," Dansforth said, who felt upset himself.

"Sidney will help him. That's what he's trained to do. Peter will soon be feeling much better."

Joy nodded in concert with the redhead and Elliot, as if to symbolize their group approval of Madeline's decision.

"Can I share now? Would that be all right?" Madeline said. "I know I'm supposed to wait till the end."

"That's what I thought," Elliot mumbled.

"But I just can't wait to tell you about my special experience of beauty, and now might be a very appropriate time."

"What was it?" Joy said. "Did you discover something?" She completely focused on Madeline's secret as if Traynor now no longer existed.

"Yes I did," she said, "The most special place of all. I found Heaven."

"Where did you go?" asked Kathy. "I want to go there too."

"I don't think you understand. I didn't go to any place that you'll find on a map. I was in the real Heaven, and *it* came to *me*."

"But isn't Heaven just s'posed to exist after you die?" Kathy said, with a puzzled look.

"I learned differently, didn't I? Now I know that Heaven isn't just a place above the clouds, it travels to us when we're ready and can appear and envelop each one of us at any moment, when we're alive, and then later after our body dies, as well. You see, the other world does things whenever it wants or knows it should."

"Did you pray very hard?" Kathy asked.

"No. I didn't pray unusually hard. At that moment I wasn't praying at all. It just came to me because it was ready and I was ready, too."

"I guess Heaven can't wait," Elliot said jokingly and everyone except Madeline laughed together for a few seconds.

"It's incredible!" said Joy.

"Yes, it really is."

"I feel bad that Peter's missing this," Dansforth said.

"Peter will hear about it. I'll make sure he knows."

"When did it happen? Where did it happen?" Elliot said.

"You know the line from the Beatles' song 'arrive without traveling'? Well, that's what happened to me because Heaven came to my apartment just three months ago. The real Heaven—the real deal."

"But how exactly did it happen?" Elliot asked, putting his glasses back on and staring hard at her.

Madeline gave him an even harder look back before her smile reappeared.

"I'd just finished taking a shower. I stepped out of the tub and reached for the towel I use to dry myself when I felt Heaven instantly and completely."

"Before you even got to the towel?" Elliot asked.

"I'm not embarrassed to say I was naked. I went to touch the towel and it was sparkling and vibrating in the same light that filled the entire room . . . and then, of course, I forgot about the towel. I looked up and the window was covered with a lemony-white light too. Though it was only open a crack, when I looked through it I could see for endless miles . . ."

"Forgive me for playing devil's advocate, ha ha," Elliot said, "but how can you be sure it wasn't just a combination of your being in an exceptionally good mood and the sunlight hitting your bathroom at a unique angle? I'm not trying to diminish your experience, it's just that when a word like *Heaven* is used, one wants to be sure, am I right?"

"Believe me, when the other world decides to visit you it makes sure you know it and, trust me, you are a thousand percent sure when it does. A lot of it, of course, can't be put into words. Our language is of the earth, so when Heaven visits the earth language can only hint at it. Do you understand, Elliot?"

Elliot nodded slowly and meaningfully as if he'd just had a profound realization. His skepticism doesn't run very deep, Dansforth noted.

"How long did the visit last?" Kathy asked. Dansforth noticed there were tears in her eyes, and one, in fact, had already freed itself and was sliding down her cheek.

"Our notions of time don't really apply to the other world. The best way I can describe it is as a completely realized moment that expands inside you. A moment that begins outside you and then is absorbed within you. In that sense, it's still going on because it's changed me forever."

Joy now began to cry softly as well.

"Is there any way, any way at all," Elliot said, gesturing rather clumsily with both hands, "that you could put into words how it's changed you or altered your perspective about what you should do now that you know Heaven exists?"

Madeline laughed. "Just to keep doing what I have been doing, only with even more dedication. That's why I'm here today sharing and listening, and when someone like Peter gets too negative, trying to help him to literally see the light . . . and find his own Heaven."

· · · · · · · · · ·

After a couple more testimonies the meeting ended, to be resumed the next morning. There was a buffet lunch in the hotel dining room, which Dansforth pretended to be going to. Instead, he returned to his room to write his notes about the session, filled with as many direct quotes as possible, before locking the material in his briefcase next to his tape recorder. The tape recorder (which was forbidden at the conference) was small enough that he was tempted to put it in his sports jacket and record tomorrow morning's session, which would certainly save a lot of work as well as being considerably more accurate. But the consequences of getting caught were far too great to justify the risk. Possibly he could use it for a one-on-one interview with some of the conference members, but that was it. He suddenly thought of interviewing Traynor, called the front desk and asked to be connected to his room, but there was no answer.

Dansforth was alarmed. Of course, Traynor could be any number of places; his failure to answer the phone hardly meant he was in peril or even still in the company of Sidney (or Dr. Refocus, as Dansforth now thought of him). Still, he couldn't rid himself of his anxieties and thought he would go to the buffet to look for him there. What he really felt like doing was going directly to Traynor's room but, of course, didn't know his room number. Maybe he could find out from someone at the buffet or, failing that, get the information out of one of the underage-looking hotel clerks.

The buffet was even more crowded than he'd imagined. The conference (which Dansforth realized had taken over most of the hotel) certainly had the Midas touch. He stood in long lines with his plate in hand to get his portion of chicken, mashed potatoes, and string beans. Nothing very beautiful about the food, he thought, which reminded him of his high-school cafeteria, but at least it would fill his empty stomach.

He felt he already needed a break from the conference so headed for the least-populated table he could find in a far corner of the room. Without even looking at who else was at the table he put down his tray and was about to seat himself when glancing, to his left, he thought he saw Traynor passing through the lobby.

Immediately he began weaving through the tray-toting members as fast as he could and managed to intercept Traynor just before he reached the door.

"Peter," Dansforth called out. "Wait a second."

Traynor squinted, looked at him for perhaps two seconds and then walked out of the hotel, suitcase in hand.

"Jesus!" Dansforth muttered as he followed him outside. Traynor was still there in front of the hotel, apparently waiting for a cab. There was a cut above Traynor's eye, a rather deep one he hadn't noticed before, and what looked like a bruise on his left cheek.

"Peter, how are you?"

Traynor half nodded then looked away.

"Could I talk to you for a minute?" Dansforth said as he walked up to him. "Are you all right? What happened with Sidney?"

"I have nothing to say about that now. I'm leaving this horror, and then I'll tell the whole world about this so-called conference. If you have half a brain you'll do the same thing."

Traynor had an extraordinary expression in his gray, bloodshot eyes—a bizarre mix of anger and anxiety—and for a moment Dansforth felt ashamed and fell silent. Before he could think of anything to say a cab pulled up with the curious name of Bat Taxi (complete with a painting of a black bat on the door) and a moment later Traynor was inside it as it pulled away.

Dansforth stood in place for a while stunned by what Traynor said, as well as by the wounds on his face, which he was almost positive weren't there before. When he looked out he saw Dr. Refocus and Madeline talking to each other in front of the hotel door and thought they were both staring at him. Finally Dansforth waved at them, but at that exact moment they turned and went inside the hotel. Only then did Dansforth shake himself loose to return to his now lukewarm lunch. It didn't follow, he reminded himself as he sat down at his table, that the cut and bruise were the result of Traynor's time spent with Dr. Refocus. Other explanations were certainly possible. Traynor was an older man and could well have slipped in the shower, bumped into a door, fallen, or hurt himself in any number of other ways—though the timing of it, as well as his rapid exit and reference to the conference as "this horror," which he was going to tell the world about, certainly made foul play the likeliest explanation. And should that even be surprising? His boss had already referred to it as the conference of lunatics, and Dansforth knew it was only one small step from lunacy to violence.

"May I join you?" said a woman's voice. Dansforth looked up and saw Madeline standing with her tray in hand.

"Of course," he said, trying to reacquire his cheerfully polite Stanley Seely tone of voice.

"Thanks. How are you enjoying the conference so far?" she said, turning toward him slightly with her inevitable smile.

"Very much. It's really been fascinating," he said, smiling back and taking the opportunity to study her for the first time. She had a pretty, roundish, blue-eyed face (an apt match in a way for her plumpish body) framed by her ostensibly natural blond hair cut fairly short and set in an old-fashioned wave. More interesting was her bright yellow low-necked summer dress and her larger than average breasts. Dansforth guessed her to be in her mid forties, a good five years older than him and so not too much of a temptation despite his ongoing status as an overly available single man.

"I was really touched by what you said," Dansforth added. "It was very moving and an incredible surprise, of course." He hoped he had sounded earnest enough, and that as a lifelong unbeliever he'd expunged every trace of sarcasm from his voice. He waited while Madeline swallowed her potatoes.

"Thanks, Stanley, that's why I shared it. I wondered if I was doing the right thing by testifying so early in our meeting when I'm supposed to be the moderator, but I guess the words just welled up and burst out of me," she said laughing.

"I'm very glad they did," Dansforth said as he negotiated his own spoonful of potatoes. "Of course, it does make me curious about certain things."

"Such as?"

"Well, it makes me want to ask you some personal questions, I suppose."

"All questions between persons are personal. Go ahead and ask."

"What was happening in your life before, you know, you . . ."

"Found Heaven?"

"Yes."

"I was a seeker just like most of the people at the conference. I was on a constant search for beauty and love and I was frustrated to a degree, both in my work and in the love part of my life."

"And now you're not," Dansforth said, almost resentfully.

"Now, of course, I've found the greatest love of all from the other world so now I know more clearly than ever what my life's work is. You see how they interconnect?"

"OK. But before, would it be fair to say you were disappointed for quite a while?"

She chewed a piece of chicken while she thought it over. Then she looked directly at him. "That would be fair to say. I'd had a divorce. It's no secret. Even the director of the conference knows about it. And my experiences meeting men after my divorce weren't always happy ones and eventually my confidence got kinda low."

Dansforth nodded supportively. "Tell me about it. I've been answering singles ads for two years now. You meet quite a parade of humanity."

"I've answered those ads too, placed them and answered them as well. You see I have no secrets, Stanley. No secrets and no shame—that's my motto, or one of them," she said, looking closely at him and laughing again.

"It's good that you can laugh about it all."

"I've gotten a lot more confident because of the other world, and you know what I discovered? When you're confident you begin to laugh again like you did as a child. It's infectious too; people pick up your confidence right away and gain confidence in you as a result. I'll give you an example from my life. Just two weeks after I found the other world I was elected the new president of Conference Operations. Coincidence or not? You tell me."

"Congratulations."

"I've gotten a lot more confident with men, too," she said, looking meaningfully at Dansforth.

"I wish I could get some of that confidence I had when I was younger," Dansforth blurted.

"I'll tell you what, Stanley. Do you have some free time tonight?"

"Sure."

"Maybe we can talk about it at dinner. I could meet you by the pool—say, at eight."

"OK, great," Dansforth said, feeling the first stirrings of an erection in spite of himself. He wanted to put a hand on her leg or better still on one of her well showcased breasts and might have done so if Elliot hadn't suddenly sat down immediately to Madeline's right, looking intense behind his black-rimmed glasses. This effect was heightened by his black jeans and black short-sleeve shirt, an anomaly among a sea of pastels.

"OK if I sit here?" he asked, half to himself it seemed.

It's a little late to be asking that, Dansforth thought. "Of course, the more the merrier," Dansforth said. Madeline turned her face to Elliot with one of her more enduring smiles. Elliot nodded then began eating rapidly, head bent down close to his plate like a bulldog. But after a few spoonfuls he surprised Dansforth by speaking directly to Madeline. "I've been thinking about what you said this morning, thinking about it a lot and I've got some questions."

"Of course, Elliot," Madeline said, with a slightly nervous expression. "What is it?"

"OK, you said you had no doubt your experience with Heaven was real."

"No doubt at all."

"I'm wondering then who you informed about it and when?"

"It informed and formed me. I felt no need to broadcast it to the world, Elliot."

"But you're telling us all now. Didn't you want to tell the press or the police right after it happened or a neighbor, at least, about the incredible thing you'd just experienced?"

"Not at all. I felt completely fulfilled and at peace and talking about it was the furthest thing from my mind."

"What about telling family or friends?"

"My family are all nonbelievers, what's left of them," she said bitterly. "My friends I did eventually tell. You're all my friends and I told you about it today, didn't I?"

"So, as the experience got less intense you decided to talk about it more. Is that it?"

"The experience didn't get less intense, I simply learned how to adjust to my newly blessed state."

"Oh," said Elliot, stroking his chin thoughtfully. "So, no one ever examined your bathroom, no professional people who might have found, say, some traces of unusual particles."

"It's not a crime scene, Elliot. Why would I want anyone to search my bathroom?" she said, forcing a laugh. "I already knew and will always know what happened. Do you see?"

Dansforth noticed then that she'd managed to finish her lunch while Elliot was talking.

"If you'll excuse me," she said, "they're some conference chores I have to do now. I'll see you later Elliot, and you I'll see tonight," she said to Dansforth with a wink before she rose, turned and walked away.

"Like a guilty thing upon a fearful summons," Elliot said, half to himself, while Dansforth, panicking slightly at the thought of being alone with him, took the opportunity to study his schedule. He noticed that he and Elliot would be in the "Weaving Beauty" seminar together in a half hour. He could always interview Elliot for the article later when everyone had free time scheduled, but right now thinking about Dr. Refocus and the director, he wanted to see where Madeline (whom he also felt strangely attracted to) was going, if it wasn't already too late.

"I'm afraid I've got to go too," said Dansforth. "I'll see you in a little while. We're in another group together."

"Sure," Elliot said nodding, his face still showing a sense of disappointed shock.

Fortunately, her hotel-wide celebrity caused Madeline to be stopped a couple of times by conference members on her way to the elevator, allowing Dansforth to catch up. He'd never had to follow a woman in any of his previous assignments and felt a vague sense of both shame and excitement. He decided to stay at a side angle about thirty feet from her, keeping his eyes on the downward progress of the twin elevators, thinking it would be too awkward and suspicious to ride with her. Instead, he thought he'd simply try to figure out, if possible, what floor she was going to. He counted three people in the elevator then looked up at the floor numbers above. There was a stop on floor two, one on floor three, then one at the Penthouse Suite. From what he'd observed about most people in power, they preferred to be separated from their minions as much as possible and if they had to be in the same hotel they preferred to be high above them. He thought Madeline's destination was almost certainly the Penthouse Suite, where he'd heard the elusive director was staying

When his elevator arrived, he pressed the Penthouse floor, regretting that he'd never gotten a good look at the director, a man named Eugene Bowers, who'd seemed football-player large from behind in his navy-blue suit. Indeed, there was only one public photograph of him in the conference catalogue, in which he was smiling atop a hill of some sort (how guru appropriate, Dansforth had thought), like a beneficent king.

There were two penthouse suites on the top floor, one at each end of the floor. Two parallel staircases led to two no-doubt-identical observation decks, where the ocean would definitely be visible. Dansforth approached the nearest suite gingerly, putting his ear to the door for nearly a full minute, but heard nothing. Perhaps his theory was incorrect. He hesitated, then walked to the other suite and listened again. This time he heard voices and then a half moaning, half yelling—either a sound of pain or some kind of agonizing sexual pleasure.

Fascinated, appalled, he listened until he was sure he heard a woman's voice that could be Madeline's followed by a man's commanding voice. But how long could he stay like that? Suddenly, checking his watch he realized that his next group discussion would begin in less than five minutes, so he quickly retreated to the elevator. When he finally reached the lobby he ripped out a piece of blank notebook paper, folded it in quarters, and carried it to the Registration Desk.

"Could I leave a message for Mr. Bowers, the director of the conference?" he asked a young brunette.

"Sure."

"He's in Penthouse B, I believe."

"Yes sir."

Dansforth handed her the blank, folded-over page.

"Would you like an envelope to put that in sir?"

"Thank you, an envelope would be great."

So the noise had come from the director's suite and may well have involved Madeline. Dansforth couldn't help shaking a little as he raced into the ballroom, where the "Weaving Beauty" seminar was held. He wanted to ask Elliot what conclusions he'd reached about Madeline's "Heaven experience" and what he knew, if anything, about Traynor. There were a number of things he wanted to speak to Elliot about, but Elliot wasn't there. His chair was empty, though his name card was present, and when Dansforth asked, no one could account for his whereabouts. Had he wandered by mistake to a different table? Dansforth stood up and slowly scanned the ballroom filled with at least fifty tables but saw no sign of him.

"We'd better begin," said Eugenie, a Chinese American woman, who Dansforth later discovered was Joy's sister. But that was about all he discovered in the group. If the morning's discussion produced a number of memorable people like Traynor, Madeline, and Elliot, each of whom seemed permanently etched into his mind, the afternoon group was a bland and oddly formless band of need-aholics mouthing a medley of clichés about "embracing energy." Nothing new for his article, that was for sure. Besides, Dansforth was distracted by his thoughts about Traynor and Madeline and now by Elliot's absence, which he thought about more the longer it lasted.

He thought he might get some relief walking along the beach and maybe wading in the water. After all, he reminded himself, his assignment was merely to write an amusing article about an absurd conference—it wasn't his charge to solve all the mysteries lurking behind its well-financed façade. Yet he knew that, while this line of thought was correct, it was also an attempt, made much too late, to fool himself. His concern was no longer just about the article. He had only to remember the look on Traynor's bruised face outside the hotel as he was leaving the conference or the harrowing symphony of screams he'd heard coming from the director's suite to realize the conference was almost certainly more sinister than absurd.

He looked up suddenly and saw a man flying in the air. It was a paraglider being pulled by a speedboat. Around the glider flew a small but broken flock of birds. One would think they'd be seagulls, but from his angle they looked to be dark birds—possibly crows. Yet how could that be possible, Dansforth wondered, as he kept walking alone away from the hotels that lined the beach until he suddenly felt oddly vulnerable, as if a telescope or worse might be targeted on him. He shuddered, then began racing across the sand back to the hotel.

By the time he reached the lobby he was hyperventilating and went directly to his room, where he lay down to get his breath back. As his breathing slowly returned to normal he realized how exhausted he was and thought he might take a nap, but he soon got up from his bed with a start and began pacing.

It was quarter to seven. He thought about the questions he wanted to ask Madeline when he saw her, and how and when he would ask them, then thought he might watch TV while he waited the last hour before their meeting.

He was watching a game show when the phone rang.

"Hello Stanley?" a woman's somewhat husky voice said.

He paused a moment before saying, "Yes, it's me."

"Hi. It's Madeline."

"Oh hi," he said, as breezily as he could manage.

"I'm afraid there's been a change of plans, and I won't be able to meet you tonight like we'd planned," she said a little shakily.

"I'm sorry," he said, wishing he were tape-recording the conversation and wondering if it was too late to do so. "Is everything all right? Are you OK?"

There was a pause before she said, "I hear intense disappointment in your voice. Did you really want to see me? Is it really important to you?"

"Yes. It is important to me. Definitely."

"Well, OK. Maybe I can see you for a few minutes then. Can you come to Room 616?

"Of course. When?"

"Can you come now?"

He told her he would leave immediately but instead sprinted into the bathroom to brush his teeth, apply some deodorant and cologne, give his private parts a sponge bath, and take a pack of condoms with him as well. He was almost out the door when he realized he'd forgotten his tape recorder, but when he went to look for it in his bag, it was missing. Had he put it somewhere else without realizing it, or remembering where? There was no more time to look; he'd kept Madeline waiting long enough. The worst thing would be if she was so angry at his tardiness that she'd cancel the meeting. She struck Dansforth as an unpredictable personality, an impulsive diva full of surprises and secrets who might do anything at any moment. Wasn't it surprising, he thought, as he got out of the elevator, that she had a room on the sixth floor among the plebeians, although it was clearly her he'd heard moaning in the Penthouse Suite.

He knocked on the door trying to compose himself.

"Who is it?" Madeline said in an anxious voice.

"It's me, Stanley."

"Oh, OK," she said, opening the door.

She was wearing big, round, dark sunglasses, which looked both sexy and slightly ridiculous.

"Come in, sit down."

He looked around, trying not to stare at her glasses, and sat by a circular Formica table near the window. She was wearing the same low-cut yellow dress she'd worn at the buffet and he tried not to stare at her cleavage, either. Wasn't that the way it always was? he thought. As soon as you become attracted to someone you tried not to stare at her, but the temptation became irresistible, like staring at a dessert you want to devour.

"Would you like a drink?" she said. "You can see I've already had one."

"Sure, whatever you're having," he said, only then noticing the bottle of gin and tonic water on the table. She poured him a glass and sat down next to him. Immediately he looked briefly at her breasts.

"OK, Stanley, I'm gonna lay my cards right on the table. I know you're attracted to me, right?"

Dansforth half shrugged and nodded.

"Ever since the other world visited me men have wanted me twice as much as before and they liked me pretty well then. I guess I have a special aura now. I think it's my Heaven dust, which sparkles and attracts even good-looking, younger men like you. I notice some women have been making passes at me lately, too. Do you believe it?"

"I believe it," Dansforth said.

"So, what I'm saying is, I know what you're feeling for me and I want to reward you," she said, sliding a hand across the table. After giving him a quick squeeze she withdrew it. "But first I need to talk to you because there are a few things on my mind and I need to find out if we're on the same page."

He nodded then said, "Of course." The sudden erection she'd produced in him was causing his mind to drift, almost guaranteeing that he wouldn't follow what she was about to say and making him wonder at the same time if what she was saying about her newfound powers from Heaven might somehow be true.

"You think loyalty is an important quality, Stanley?"

"Loyalty? Sure."

"And do you think if two people make love then there ought to be a bond of loyalty between them?"

"Ideally, yes."

"Good, we're definitely on the same page. We're like a couple of sentences nestled together in the same paragraph, so far. Me, I think loyalty is really important. But, even loyalty, except to God, has its limits. Loyalty has to first be inspired, but to keep it you have to earn it, you have to follow through and be the kind of person you presented yourself as at the start. You notice the sunglasses I'm wearing? Have you figured out why I'm still wearing them indoors?"

"I wouldn't want to speculate."

"Because the man I was loyal to crossed the line on me and now I'm not so pretty to look at, around my eyes."

There was a choking in her voice. Then she finished her drink and poured herself another. As a sign of solidarity (among other reasons) Dansforth also finished his and embarked on his second drink almost immediately. "Is there anything I can do to help you?" he said.

"The other world is already helping me, but thanks for the offer. Listen, have you noticed that the conference has been changing? Come on, admit it, I know you have."

"Yes, I've noticed, from what I've been told, that there's been a shift of emphasis . . ."

"What kind of emphasis?"

"From the purely aesthetic to the confessional."

"You left out the last stage that leadership planned, you left out the spiritual. But these changes are a good thing—or were when we planned them."

Dansforth felt his heart beat. So Madeline was more than just a newly elected president and membership organizer. She was a kind of co-director or at least the director's partner in more ways than he'd heard outside the penthouse.

"Art and beauty *should* make people think and talk about themselves, should lead them to confession—to use your word—until the point when they're ready for a higher world, as I was when I experienced Heaven. That was the vision the leadership created and that we were all loyal to. The problem is, a very powerful person in the organization had a different idea and started practicing it. He believes that certain . . . ah, sexual practices he favors have great spiritual value and should be mandatory among all the members, and I found that I couldn't accept his vision. Are you following me?"

Dansforth nodded, as she started yet another drink. "You sure you follow me? The world is burning and there isn't much time. Here, feel my breasts," she said, leaning forward. "No, not on my dress, feel my God-stunned flesh. Go on, feel them, hold them."

Dansforth did as instructed until after a few seconds she pulled away.

"Now the other world is over your fingers, now my Heaven dust is in your body forever. That's enough of a gift, wouldn't you say?"

Dansforth looked at her but said nothing.

"Remember the world is burning and dark forces are stalking the land. There's very little time."

"For us tonight?"

"Yes, and for you in particular."

"What do you mean?"

"OK. I'm gonna put another pack of cards on the table. I know who you are, or should I say, who you aren't."

"What do you mean?"

"Come on now, don't be coy with me after I let you feel my Heaven dust. I know you're not Stanley Seely, that's just a name you're using."

Dansforth looked down at the table.

"More important, *they* know who you are."

"Who knows? How?"

"You weren't very careful who you were seen talking to, for one thing, and you were even less careful who you were seen listening to. There are security cameras on the ceiling of the penthouse floor, my friend, and you were seen spying at the wrong door for a very long time. So people began looking into you on the Internet. They know that Stanley Seely is dead, though you do have a kind of frightening resemblance to him. They know you have a tape recorder, too, which our rules explicitly forbade you to bring to the conference. They figure you're a reporter planning some exposé and that your bosses gave you the ID. They're planning to have a Truth or Consequences session with you soon."

"When?"

"Very soon. That's why I say there's not much time, not even time to make love, because you need to leave this conference as soon as possible or . . . well . . ."

"The same thing that happened to Traynor and maybe Elliot too will happen to me?"

"Those are your words, not mine. Don't be angry with me. I didn't have to tell you any of this and, of course, you're not to repeat any of what I told you to anyone—are you clear about that? Especially not in your article, or some really bad stuff will happen to you—stuff even the other world couldn't help you with."

Her voice, which had been so invitingly erotic a little while ago, now seemed laced with contempt.

"You look confused. You have a confused look on your face, like Alice in Wonderland. I hope what I'm saying is sinking in. Look Stanley, or whatever your name is, you're a cute guy and I'm attracted to you on the one hand, but I don't like spies and snitches on the other. But, I'm going to give you a break, so listen carefully to this, these are my last words to you: pack up your things and leave this conference and forget about your article. But, if you do have to write something, just write a gently amusing piece. You can make a little fun of people at the conference but make your overall piece kind of positive. Otherwise, you'll find that the conference has a long arm. You'll find it's like a giant octopus with eight very long arms and lots of legs and that it will hunt you down and find you and then deal with you in a very hurtful way. You've already got a dead man's ID, Stanley, you don't want his future too, do you?"

Dansforth felt himself shake for a moment, then got up unsteadily from the table. He looked straight at Madeline's sunglasses and said, "Are we done?"

"*We're* done, but Sidney and a few other of the director's men are coming to this room for you in less than five minutes."

Dr. Refocus, Dansforth thought to himself and felt a tremor pass through him. He was still too angry to run in front of her so he walked steadily for the most part till he got to the door, resisting the temptation to look back at her as he closed it.

I have the mind of an investigator but I definitely don't have the heart of one, he thought, as he ran down the three flights of stairs to his room. He packed in less than a minute, intentionally leaving his toilet articles and some other things, in case they searched his room again and might conclude he was still in the hotel. There would be no time to check out. Instead he'd leave by the side exit that led to the pool (where he was originally supposed to meet Madeline), walk out to the beach, and then cross over to a neighboring hotel, where he could get a cab. He wasn't going to make himself a sitting duck like Traynor had and probably Elliot, too.

He took one last quick look at the sea as he ran and thought he saw a fish jumping—a dolphin perhaps—but there was no time to double-check so he couldn't be sure.

Later, in the cab riding toward the Tampa airport, he thought of that ambiguous fish as a metaphor for journalism in general. Like the fish he couldn't identify, there was never enough time to know what you really saw, much less to understand it. He knew now that he had to eventually leave the paper. Better to give his boss a "gently amusing story," which Madeline had told him to do in the room, then start looking for a better job, or at least a different one.

As he hurried to the ticket counter (he'd have to pay an extra hundred, of course, for taking an earlier flight) Dansforth saw an unusually large number of men in police and medical uniforms, but kept moving forward without asking any questions. It wasn't until he was back in the office of his St. Louis apartment the next morning looking at the St. Petersburg paper on the Internet that he discovered why so many police had been there. He read a story about a man who'd killed himself in the same part of the Tampa airport Dansforth had walked through just hours later.

As he read on he was horrified to learn that the deceased was his colleague from the seminar, Peter Traynor, who'd apparently overdosed on sleeping pills in the men's room, although there was some speculation that foul play might have been involved. In the newspaper photograph taken from an earlier time in his life, Traynor looked relatively composed, the way a philanthropist and connoisseur of beauty might be expected to look. Not at all like Dansforth's last memory of his face. While he studied the photograph on the Internet, Dansforth unconsciously picked up a copy of his article from his desk until it began to shake in his hands. Then he stood up and dropped it as if it were a rattlesnake. The article lay on the floor face up. Dansforth stared at it, kicked it hard once, moving the pages a few feet, then started pacing around it in circles saying over and over to himself, "I'm going to call in sick today, I'm going to call in sick."

Fiction Titles in the Series